From

Denise Domning

PRAISE FOR
SERVANT OF THE CROWN **MYSTERIES**

"Domning brings the English country-side alive with all the rich detail of a Bosch painting. CSI 12th century style. I can't wait to see more."

— Christina Skye, *New York Times* best-selling author of *A Highlander for Christmas*

"Pure and unapologetically Medieval. Five solid stars."

— Kathryn LeVeque, best-selling author of *The Wolfe*

THE DEAD WALK!

It's the time of year when the immortal army of the ancient king appears on Watling Street and the dead become uneasy in their graves. Indeed, in the far north of Warwickshire, the villagers insist that one dead man returned to kill his only son. Now it's up to Sir Faucon de Ramis, the shire's new Crowner, to run the walking corpse to ground and put him back where he belongs.

Other Books

Dedication

To all of the my farm animals, past and present. I've learned so much about life from them, and so much more about death.

My Apologies

My apologies to the people of Warwickshire. I have absconded with your county, added cities that don't exist and parsed your history to make it suit my needs. Outside of that, I've done my best to keep my recreation of England in the 12th Century as accurate as possible.

caught red-handed

DENISE
DOMNING

CAUGHT RED-HANDED

Copyright © Denise Domning 2019

ISBN-13: 978-1704077802
:

EDITED BY: Martha Stites and Kimberly Spina

ORIGINAL COVER ART: Denise Domning, Skeleton image © The British Library Board

Printed in the United States of America, First paperback edition: November, 2019

horarium
(the hours)

Matins	12:00 midnight
Lauds	3:00 A.M.
Prime	6:00 A.M.
Terce	9:00 A.M.
Sext	12:00 noon
None	3:00 P.M.
Vespers	6:00 P.M.
Compline	9:00 P.M.

St. Clement's Day

"Mother, I fear I bring bad tidings," I say as I step inside the prioress's private chamber. Bad tidings for her, but proof to me that His hand is yet at work in my life. As has happened so often before, once again a path has appeared before me. I have faith that the way will be made clear.

Seated at the far side of the room, Mother Superior raises her head to look at me. The midday sun fills the narrow arched windows behind her. Despite waxed linen panels meant to stymie the cold air, the light is bright enough to reveal flecks of white in her gray habit, the dress of our house. Her bleached linen wimple gleams, lending her a halo she does not deserve and will never earn.

Her expression tightens as she recognizes me, and her blue eyes narrow. Only as I stop at the forward edge of the table between us does she set aside the garment she's been decorating. It's a bishop's chasuble. She's adding embroidered crosses done in precious silver thread. Bracing her elbows on the arms of her chair of state, she steeples her fingers in front of her. Her brusque nod gives me permission to speak.

"Mea culpa, Mother. I at last began preparations for our Christmas festivities only to discover that I've made an unexpected error," I confess without shame. I know well my value here. My ability to tally numbers and manage the necessities of communal life has driven back the threat of dissolution. "We haven't enough candles in store to decorate for the season. But I've just come from Sister Martine, who tells me her bees have suffered this year. The hive can afford to lose no more wax."

As I fall silent, I fold my hands before me and bow my head. It takes all my will not to flinch with the movement. The cuts upon my back tighten as they heal. Sister Infirmaress offered salves to soften them, but I welcome the pain. It keeps me ever-present to what lies ahead for me, and for the child who will be my final companion.

"This cannot be," Mother Superior replies in dismay. As always happens when she's disappointed, her voice quavers so badly that her words are almost unintelligible.

"How can we celebrate the Angels Mass without candles?" she complains like a heart-sick child. Midnight mass on Christmas always finds our chapel decorated with so many candles that it seems the stars themselves hang from our ceiling.

"All is not lost, Mother," I assure her. "If our bees have suffered, the rest of our house has prospered. Although there is not enough in our purse to purchase all the wax we need for the full twelve nights, there is coin enough to provide candles for both the Angels Mass and Christmas Day. Sister Martine believes there are a number of farmsteads and hamlets nearby from which we can buy what we need. With your permission I'd visit these places, doing so soon, before the weather turns for the worse." As I speak, I raise my head far enough to watch her.

"You?" the prioress spits back, her brow creased in sharp surprise. "You've barely recovered. Send Sister Martine if she knows where these apiaries and their keepers are."

"Knowledge is one thing, Mother. Courage is another," I reply. "Who within these walls is brave enough to venture so far beyond our sanctuary walls? None save me and Sister Herbalist, and she is away until spring. That is, unless you wish to do the chore," I add to drive home my point.

Just as I expect, a shaft of fear darts through the prioress's eyes at my suggestion. I continue swiftly to take advantage of that emotion. "Although I am not yet quick on my feet, I mend rapidly. Moreover, Sister Infirmaress has recommended walking as part of my cure. Nor will I be alone. Simon will travel with me as always."

And, as always, Simon will plan to part ways with me outside of our walls, he staying with his family until I rejoin him there. It is an equitable arrangement. I prefer to travel alone and he prefers not to travel with me. Like most men, he finds me disturbing.

That piques a hopeful sound from the prioress. "Of course! Simon. He can do the task," she almost cries.

"You would trust our purse to a servant?" I reply, my brows raised.

Although there is only one sensible reply she can give to my question, I expect further argument. Instead, as if even so short a conversation with me has exhausted her, the prioress's shoulders sag. With that gesture, I see His hand sweeping the way clear for me. I give thanks to the One who arranges our lives to suit His needs.

"Mother, if you're concerned for me, allow me to take a companion, one who has already shown her willingness to support me in my recovery. Lady Marianne of Blacklea, the child who found me in my extremis. Many thanks to you for allowing her frequent visits," I offer.

"It was at her request," the prioress replies. If her tone is flat, her expression says I've confused her.

"So she has confessed," I respond with a nod. "During our time together I've come to know her as a girl of fine character with a quick mind, one fit for tallying. Were she to so choose, and with me to train her, she would make a fine cellaress. Perhaps if she and I spend more time together, she might be encouraged to consider joining us in our life instead of one outside our walls?"

As I speak, I raise my head even farther until I am looking directly at my superior. Astonishment adds wrinkles to the prioress's already creased face. She's never once heard me attempt to promote our house, and she's certainly never seen me show any interest in our students. Almost immediately, her surprise melts into avarice, just as I knew it must. Lady Marianne has kin in Coventry, a family of well-to-do cloth merchants.

Won over by the thought of exploiting the child's rich connections, the prioress nods. "I will agree to this," she says. "Remember that the child is our responsibility. Even with Simon to guard you, you and she cannot be away from our walls after nightfall."

"Of course not," I agree. "None of the places Sister Martine mentioned are far, but it would tax me to try to visit them all in one day. Instead, Lady Marianne and I will make several short trips. If you allow, there's enough day left to this afternoon that we could make our first foray, going only as far as the baker in the village. Sister Martine says he always has wax to spare."

Stark amazement rounds my superior's eyes. Her mouth opens. "You, who ever chides us for celebrating our saints with aught but quiet meditation, would deign to walk among the commoners on Saint Clement's Day?"

Today we celebrate the second bishop of Rome, Clement, the man who followed Saint Peter onto that holy throne and who was martyred by the pagan Emperor Trajan. Rather than contemplating the sacrifices made by those who built our Church, the commoners —especially the smiths— have turned this day into one of mindless merriment.

"Mother, you're wrong. I do not judge others," I tell her. "I have always recognized that my practices are but one way to worship our Lord. However, I find such peace and joy in how I worship that I wish only to share it with others. You must recall that I was an infant oblate and this life—" the lift of my hand is meant to include the whole of our house "—is the only life I've ever known. The customs of the laity will ever and always be strange to me.

"As for Lady Marianne," I continue, "she is no doubt well-accustomed to such raucous revelry. I thought an outing on this day might be a way to show my gratitude for her care and kindness."

Again, the prioress gapes at me. Disbelief fair wafts from

her. I hold my breath. Her mouth snaps shut and she offers a slow and approving nod.

"Perhaps it is possible for you to change, Daughter," she says, a tiny smile pulling at her full lips. "Know that kindness and tolerance become you. I pray this is not the last time you will reveal them to me. Thus, with hope for both your and Lady Marianne's future among us, I agree to your request."

I offer her a quick bend of my knees. "Have no fear for the child. She and I are safe in our Lord's hands."

Chapter One

"But sir, you cannot tell them this was an accidental death," Brother Edmund insisted.

Although the day's clear sky and bright sun had turned a frosty morning into a mild afternoon, the monk still had the cowl of his black habit pulled close around his well-made face. As Edmund spoke he gave a sweep of his hand to indicate the fish pond that the dead man had been hired to help expand, the same place where he had taken his fatal injury.

"Even though it was several days before the man perished," continued the clerk who served Warwickshire's newly-elected Coronarius, "by all rights the tool should be named deodand, for murder was most definitely done."

The twelve Cistercians arranged around their spiritual kinsman stirred uneasily at this. As one, they looked at Brother Edmund's employer. Sir Faucon de Ramis cursed himself. Would that he'd known all the circumstances of the man's death before he'd begun his northward journey to Merevale Abbey. Faucon was certain he'd still have come, doing so for no other reason than to introduce himself where he was yet a stranger. However, had he known that the injury had occurred on Church land, he'd have left Brother Edmund to his priory and his prayers.

Then Faucon expanded his curse to include Sir Alain, Warwickshire's sheriff. The sheriff's latest attempt to rid his shire of its new servant of the crown had doomed Faucon to riding out dressed in full armor, his gambeson beneath his chain mail tunic and leggings, with his shield on his saddle and his metal helmet on his head. Despite the cool air, the sun was strong. By noon Faucon had felt overheated, but all he dared remove was his helmet and his chain mail hood. Even now sweat trickled down his spine.

"Brother Edmund," he said to his clerk, shrugging to ease the prickle, "we have verified the wound that killed the man occurred on abbey land. His death isn't ours to investigate. Why does it matter what I say?"

"But sir, it does matter!" Brother Edmund protested, his brown eyes widening as if his employer's response had astonished him. An earnest crease formed between his brows. "You know as well as I that precision is of the utmost importance when it comes to death and the law."

Standing at Faucon's left, his brother Sir William de Ramis freed a scoffing breath. Will was also fully armed and had shed his headgear earlier in their ride. Although Faucon's brother was two years Faucon's senior, silver already threaded his hair and glinted at his temples. Except for that, he and Faucon were startlingly similar in appearance, sharing the same thick black hair, broad brow, lean cheeks, and long nose. The resemblance was reinforced by the fact that they both chose to wear a closely-trimmed beard to hide what they agreed was a too-pointed chin.

Alf, the common soldier Faucon paid to watch his back, stood slightly behind Will. The tall fair-haired Englishman was also armed, dressed in a boiled leather hauberk studded with metal rings. Like his betters, he also wore a sword belted at his side. Alf had his arms crossed in front of him. His brimmed metal helmet hung from one elbow by its leather strap. As the common soldier caught his employer's glance, he gave an amused lift of his brows.

"Moreover, these are Cistercians," Edmund was saying. "Sir, Cistercians have no learning. You must take care to be clear or you'll confuse them."

This time Will choked on his laughter. Faucon groaned inwardly. Worse and worse!

He stepped between Edmund and Merevale's abbot. "My

lord, I pray you forgive my clerk," he begged of Abbot Henry. The well-born Churchman was a small, clean-shaven man. With the afternoon so warm, he'd pushed back his cowl. The day's breeze made free with his curling, grizzled hair, setting it to dancing around his plain face. Gentle amusement filled the abbot's hazel eyes. The corners of his mouth quirked.

"The law is Brother Edmund's passion," Faucon continued, "and he is particular about its application. But I take his instruction, and will be clear. My clerk is correct. If the injury had been taken beyond your boundaries, I would name the tool deodand and call the jury to pronounce murder. But the man was injured on your land. This makes the matter your or your bishop's concern, not mine or our king's."

"Have no fear, Sir Faucon," Henry of Merevale replied in their shared French tongue. "Learning weighs heavily on our Benedictine brothers and we are happy to let them bear that weight. I assure you that the shovel does indeed belong to the abbey. We have prayed daily since the accident to cleanse all stain from both the offending tool and our home."

Edmund breathed out in noisy relief. "That is well done, Father Abbot."

"Thank you, Brother," his better replied with no trace of sarcasm.

Then the abbot again looked at Faucon. "It seems I must beg your pardon, sir. It was Atherstone's headman who insisted that you be called after Thomas's death. He tells me that it is you, not our sheriff, that he must now summon in the matter of unnatural death. He says our sheriff no longer has the right to assemble the inquest jury."

Here, the abbot paused to tilt his head in question. "What is it the headman called you? A Crowner?" He rolled the English word on his tongue as if testing its pronunciation.

"Sir Faucon is more correctly addressed as Coronarius," Brother Edmund swiftly replied, using the Latin word for Faucon's position. "It means—"

"Servant of the crown," translated the supposedly untutored Cistercian just as swiftly, nodding to Edmund.

Faucon's clerk straightened with a start, blinking in surprise. "Exactly so."

"I was not always a Cistercian, Brother," the abbot replied with a smile, the movement of his hand indicating his undyed, woolen habit. Although an abbot, his habit was as well used as those worn by his flock. The hems of his sleeves were frayed. Patches marked the places where his knees met the floor, or the ground when he worked in the abbey's fields and gardens. Unlike the Benedictines, who spent their days surrounded by manuscripts and quills, the Cistercians— even their abbots— daily put hand to hoe or crook to provide food for their house.

This time, Will made no attempt to hide his laughter. Faucon cringed. The sound had an all-too-familiar edge to it. A decade ago his brother had taken a blow to the head that rendered him unconscious for days. When Will had finally awakened, it had been as not-Will, a man who looked and talked like Faucon's brother but wasn't at all the same man. Although Will had recently been given a potion that eased his constant head pain, he resisted taking it, complaining he couldn't sleep away his life.

"Crowner is the title by which the common men of the hundreds prefer to address me," Faucon told the abbot. "However, the more fitting title for my new position is Keeper of the Pleas. At the command of king and court, I employ Brother Edmund to see that all pleas for royal justice are inscribed on parchment, then kept safe until they can be presented to the king's justices.

"But you are correct, my lord. Our sheriff no longer investigates unnatural deaths, or charges of burglary or rape, or calls the inquest jury. Those are my duties now." Faucon didn't add that the king's councilors believed his premier duty was that of assessing and recording the value of the estates belonging to those charged with these royal crimes. Faucon's appraisal would then be used to calculate the fine the king could collect from the wrongdoer's estate.

"Huh," said Abbot Henry, his thick gray brows rising as he considered his new Crowner. Bright intelligence filled his gaze. "I think Sir Alain cannot have been much pleased by this change."

Faucon's chain mail rattled musically as he shrugged. "I wouldn't know, my lord. Although I will one day inherit land in this shire through my dam, my father's estate is in Essex. I am only now coming to know Warwickshire and its sheriff." That was true enough. However, the little Faucon did know about Sir Alain was the very reason Warwickshire's sheriff was determined to end the life of his new Coronarius by whatever means possible.

Once again, the corners of the Churchman's mouth quirked. As if he meant to hide his amusement, the abbot glanced skyward. "The sun tells me that it's near to None and that means our dinner hour is at hand. Sir Faucon, you and your party will, of course, join us for the meal. So too must you bide the night here. It's the least we can do to repay you for coming so far for no cause.

"I promise it will be worth your while," the abbot continued, smiling openly at his Crowner this time. "Brother Augustine" —he nodded toward the tallest of his flock— "has dedicated his life to producing cider. We all agree that his perry this year is his masterwork!"

While the other monks grinned and nodded in agreement, the abbey's brewmaster blushed. That had Faucon grinning as well. Unlike the rigorous life of the scholarly Benedictines, the simple honesty of the Cistercians' life spoke to him.

"My lord, there's no need to beg my pardon," he said. "I'm honored to have made your acquaintance."

Now, that was the absolute truth. The more powerful men that Faucon knew in this shire, the more influential men who knew him, the harder it became for Sir Alain to strike.

"Nor will this be a wasted trip," Faucon continued. "When my chatelaine learned I was bound for Merevale, she begged me to visit Nuneaton, which, she informs me, is not far from here.

I'm to convey her love to her daughter, who is a student with the sisters."

"That you shall do and easily so," Abbot Henry replied, looking truly pleased at this news. "Your chatelaine is correct. Nuneaton is but a way and a bit to the east of us.

"Come, then," the Churchman said, turning his back on the fish ponds and death as he stepped down into the deeply-worn path that crossed the abbey's lands.

The track, exactly wide enough to accommodate a small wagon, began at the abbey's fish ponds, then wound its snaking way between the fields that fed the monks and the pastures where their sheep grazed. While some of their fields presently rested under the stubbled remains of this autumn harvest, a surprising number showed signs of having been recently turned. These stretches of land sported sweet green lines that spoke of new growth. This could only be those vegetables— turnips, cabbages, onions and garlic— that did well during the colder months.

Beyond the newly-planted fields was a sharp lift of land dotted with rows of carefully pruned and now-barren fruit trees. As the path reached the hillside, it zigzagged up its side to the top, where the monks had built their church and home.

A movement in the track just below the hilltop caught Faucon's eye. He squinted. It was a sway-backed brown nag making its way down toward the fields. The beast moved no faster than a walking man, perhaps because it carried two. The man holding the reins wore a commoner's white linen cap. His tunic had once been a bright green, but now showed brown and rusty orange spots, his chausses were a faded red. The second man wore no cap. His wild dark-red hair stood out around his head and his brown gown was pulled high onto his thighs, revealing yellow stockings.

"Huh, more visitors. How unusual," Abbot Henry said from where he walked in the track ahead of both his flock and his guests. "Brother Samuel," the Churchman called without turning his head, "run forward and see what business these two have with us."

A fair-haired youth barely old enough to shave raised the skirt of his habit and stepped up out of the path onto the still-green verge. As the young monk raced toward the hillside, Faucon followed him onto the verge then strode quickly forward until he walked alongside, and a little above, the abbot.

"Should I accompany the brother, my lord?" he asked. The Churchman offered his new Crowner a quick wink. "I hardly think there's any need for that. What sort of threat can anyone pose to us on a day when we're accompanied by two knights and a soldier?" His tone suggested he was a man fully supported by his faith.

Rather than retreat to his previous place behind the monks, Faucon continued walking along the rough verge, matching the abbot's pace as he watched Brother Samuel. The monk was fleet of foot, for he was already a quarter of the way up the hillside while the descending nag had yet to reach the halfway point. Just then the red-headed rider slid off the horse's rump. Only as he came to earth and his dark tunic fell into place, its hem reaching to his shoes, did Faucon recognize him as a priest.

Waving frantically, the distant clergyman raced down toward the oncoming monk. When monk and priest met, the stranger grabbed Brother Samuel by the arms. Almost immediately the young monk broke free of the clergyman's hold to turn in the track.

"Father, he speaks no French," he shouted down to his abbot, his distant call faint but audible.

"Then return to us," Abbot Henry shouted back, his hands cupped to his mouth.

"If you will, my lord," Faucon said to the abbot, "my man and I will go ahead to discover what brings your visitors here." Although he formed this as a question, to his mind, seeking the abbot's permission was but a formality.

"With my blessings," Abbot Henry nodded.

Faucon turned to look at Alf. The common soldier had

already stepped up onto the verge from where he walked at the very back of their party. "Alf, at all speed," he commanded in French.

"As you will, sir," the Englishman replied with a nod.

As Alf trotted toward him along the verge, Faucon stepped down into the track in front of the abbot. He jogged, his mail jangling in tune with his jolting pace. Being less burdened by the accoutrements of war, Alf swiftly passed by his employer.

On the hillside, the English priest put a hand to his brow as he looked down upon them. Realizing that others came, he threw himself into motion, rushing pell-mell down the track after Brother Samuel. Such frantic haste only spurred Faucon to greater speed.

Alf and Brother Samuel met near the base of the hill and traded positions, the monk leaping onto the verge while the soldier stepped down into the track. A moment later the wild-haired clergyman and tall commoner met. Just as the priest had with Brother Samuel, he grabbed Alf by the forearms. And just like the monk before him, Alf tore free from the man's hold. He turned to look back at his employer just as Brother Samuel trotted past Faucon.

"Sir, it's not English he's speaking," Alf called. "I cannot understand him either."

That had Faucon lifting his heels until he sprinted. Then it was his turn to have the priest's surprisingly strong hands clasped around his forearms. The red-headed man was a little taller than Faucon and, unlike most clergymen who were clean-shaven, wore a full beard that was only a slightly lighter shade of red than his hair.

Everything about him— his grasp on Faucon's arms, his tense shoulders, his narrow, long-featured face, and his pale gray eyes— radiated urgency. His mouth opened. Sounds that might have been words tumbled from his lips. Although Faucon considered himself almost fluent in the commoners' tongue, having learned the language at his nurse's knee, not one syllable this man uttered made sense to him.

"I don't understand you," he complained, pulling his arms free of the clergyman's grasp. "Can you speak English?"

That won a groan of frustration from the priest. Faucon looked at Alf, who had retreated to the verge. "What of you? Did you understand any of what he just said?"

"Some of it sounded familiar, but I can't say I understood anything," Alf said with a shake of his head. "I'm thinking he must be a Northerner. I've never met any myself, but I'm told that when they speak the common tongue, they do it in a way that is oddly twisted."

Once again Faucon faced the priest. He lifted a hand to point up the track at the horse and rider, now but a furlong or so away. "Does that other man speak English?"

Instantly the priest pivoted in the track. "Waddard!" he shouted. "Halpa min. Spaak firr ek."

That this Waddard gave a quick nod said he had no trouble understanding his clergyman. Using only his left heel the commoner gave his mount a few quick kicks. The bony horse responded with a sorry snort but no additional speed. That one-sided kick had Faucon studying the mounted commoner more closely. It wasn't the lack of a saddle that had Waddard perched awkwardly atop his horse. Instead Faucon guessed that the man had injured his right hip, and that he walked with great pain if he walked at all.

"Sir knight, you must help us," the commoner called to him in perfectly understandable English. "I am Waddard, potter of Mancetter, and he is Father Godin, our priest. We've come to beg urgent aid from the abbot. He must stop them."

"Stop who?" Faucon called back, grateful to hear words he understood, even if they didn't quite make sense.

"My son Dickie is dead—"

Waddard of Mancetter choked off into silence, then cleared his throat and tried again. "My son Dickie is dead, and my neighbors are set on cutting his body into pieces before night-fall."

Faucon's eyes widened. Alf took a startled step back and

nearly fell from the verge into the deep track. "Sir," he gasped as he caught himself, "there's only one reason to cut apart a dead man."

"I know," Faucon replied grimly. Folk only quartered the dead when a corpse refused to stay in its grave.

Chapter Two

Faucon turned in the track. Brother Samuel had just rejoined the other monks behind their abbot in the pathway. Behind the Cistercians, both Brother Edmund and Will leaned to one side as they walked, seeking to better see what occurred in front of them.

"My lord abbot," Faucon shouted, "these two men have come from a village called Mancetter. They wish you to return with them to prevent their neighbors from cutting a dead boy into pieces."

The abbot jerked to a stop, his hand flying to the wooden cross that hung from a leather thong around his neck. His flock halted behind him, fluttering and flapping. Some moaned. Others dropped to sit on the edge of the verge. Then, almost as one, eleven of the Merevale brothers folded their hands and began to chant out a prayer of protection from evil.

Rather than bow his head along with his spiritual cousins, Brother Edmund clambered onto the verge. Skirting the monks, Faucon's clerk moved toward his employer at what was almost a run for him. Will followed just as quickly.

As Edmund halted next to Alf, the monk glanced to the opposite verge as if considering leaping across the track. He took too long in his deliberation. Will stepped over the pathway and claimed the spot. For good reason. It offered an unobstructed view of both Faucon and the men from Mancetter. Eyes narrowed, Brother Edmund turned a shoulder to the two soldiers and looked at his employer.

"Sir," he said, "I think we shouldn't be surprised to hear such news. Indeed, I'm thinking we should have already encountered other such instances since our arrival here."

"Instances? Of the dead walking?! How so?" Faucon retorted, startled by his clerk's unexpected and all-too-calm pronouncement.

"Because where Herla's army rides," Edmund began.

"The dead are uneasy in their grave," Alf completed in astonishment, his eyes wide. "How do you know of Herla?" the English soldier demanded of the Norman monk. Edmund ignored his question.

"Herla?" Faucon glanced between them. "Who is Herla?"

It was Alf who answered. "An ancient king. He leads his retainers in a ceaseless ride, for as long as they never dismount, they have eternal life."

"Exactly so," Edmund agreed brusquely without looking at the commoner. "The English call him Herla, but our tales speak of him as Harlequin."

"Holy Mother save us! Harlequin is real?" Will gasped out, crossing himself.

Faucon did the same. First the walking dead and now Harlequin? Their mother had happily terrified both her sons with tales of the gigantic, unholy man who carried a massive mace and led an army of the walking dead.

"Indeed he is, Sir William," Brother Edmund assured the knight, speaking directly to Faucon's brother for the first time since Will's arrival in Warwickshire. "And indeed we should all be begging our Lord's holy mother to aid us, if what these commoners have told Sir Faucon is true."

Both Will and Alf stared at the monk in unguarded and horrified interest. As for Faucon, he felt as though the ground beneath his feet was tilting and turning.

"As to why, I think we should not be surprised, sir," Edmund continued, turning his attention back on Faucon, "Herla's influence is strongest here in the north. I have it on good authority that he and his army are often seen riding Watling Street." As he said this, the monk gave a jerk of his head as if to indicate the ancient road that cut across England.

Shocked beyond speech, Faucon could but stare at his clerk. How could a monk— or any man for that matter— speak so sensibly of such supernatural and unsensible evil? The urge to sit on the verge and pray along with Merevale's monks filled him. He might have done it, except one tiny certainty lifted out of his spinning thoughts.

Edmund couldn't possibly know where Watling Street lay from here, not when they were both new in this shire and this was their first visit so far north in Warwickshire.

In all truth, Faucon also had no idea know where Watling Street lay. All he knew was that the Street began at Wroxeter in the north of the Welsh Marches, then angled southeastward until it reached London, from whence it proceeded to Richborough and the sea. If Edmund couldn't know that much, how could he say he knew who or what might walk on the Street?

The earth steadied beneath Faucon's feet. "Who is this authority you so trust?" he demanded. "And how is it you know anything about what happens here? You said you hailed from the south."

"And so I do," Brother Edmund replied with a nod. "I'm from London, for the most part. It was while I was in Paris studying at the university—"

"You studied at the university in Paris?!" Faucon burst out in abject surprise, certainty slipping from his fingers as the earth again began to shift.

A dead man's corpse had killed his living son, Harlequin's army was real and walked here in this shire, and the man who served him as a menial clerk had been educated in the most prestigious university in all Europe. But that was impossible. Edmund had once inferred that he was bastard-born. Only the richest noblemen sent their sons and wards to Paris. Everyone else attended the school in Oxford— where Faucon's father would have sent him had Will not been injured— which wasn't even a chartered university. What great man had opened his purse on Edmund's behalf?

"Yes, in Paris, both before and after the ban. I received my master of the arts there." His clerk gave a casual shrug as if having been accorded the second highest degree a scholar might achieve was no great thing. "As I was saying, while in Paris I met a man, another cleric, who was then in service to my—our country as an ambassador. Master Walter had formed an interest in the reanimated dead after reading the tale of a man who met Hellequin—"

"Hellequin?" Alf asked.

"Another pronunciation of Harlequin," Edmund said, again shooting the soldier a disapproving glance for daring to interrupt a second time. Then, clearing his throat, the monk shifted until he stood a little in front of the commoner.

"Master Walter was astonished to learn of a man who had encountered the army of the dead and interacted with one of the walking corpses, and managed to survive. That set him on a quest to collect any and all similar tales while he journeyed between the courts of foreign kings and bishops. Once Master Walter had collected as many tales as he could, he approached the masters of the university in Paris, seeking a copyist. Although I was but a student at the time, my mentors recommended me. I ultimately made Master Walter six copies of his collection.

"Years later, after I returned to England and had taken my vows, Master Walter again sought me out, once more in need of a copyist. This time, the tales in his collection had come from our own land, many of them originating from this area and farther north, on into the Marches. He was very grateful when I again agreed to scribe for him. Before he had located me, he'd approached a number of my brethren, as well as some unaffiliated clerks. None were willing to aid him. He told me they all refused to read, much less copy, such tales."

Edmund's lips twisted in scorn. "Ignorant, fearful fools! As if words on parchment are anything more than just words! Nor can the act of copying a word call forth whatever it is that word describes. Just as with prayer, there must be intent.

"Moreover," the monk continued, scorn giving way to

satisfaction, "they should have realized that the copies would be housed in the library at Hereford. Bishop William has long been Master Walter's patron. But you must know that, sir, what with the bishop being your uncle? You must know that your lord uncle has long had a fondness for good stories well told, and is a patron to any man who can tell them."

This time Faucon's jaw loosened. He once more stared at his clerk, stunned beyond speaking. A dozen questions arose, all of them more personal than he had a right to pose or that Brother Edmund might tolerate from him. No wonder the monk had called clerking for Warwickshire's new Crowner a penance. And no wonder Edmund was frantic to win Bishop William's forgiveness for whatever wrong he'd done that resulted in his demotion. So well educated a man must find riding out daily to deal with backward commoners in these backward hundreds akin to burning in hell.

When his employer continued to stare at him, Edmund cocked his head a little. "Sir, gather your wits. You must pay heed, for this is very important." His tone was that of master to student. "You must ask these men how many in their village have been visited by the dead man's corpse. Of those who have seen the abomination, how many have fallen ill?"

Both Edmund's question and his manner cut through Faucon's spinning thoughts. He sucked in a deep breath, feeling as if he were rising out of a dream. "Let me ask them," he told his clerk, then again faced the track and the commoners waiting in it.

Waddard of Mancetter had brought his nag to a halt a few feet behind his Northern priest. Honest grief expressed openly had left dirty tracks on the potter's plump cheeks. As he realized he had his Crowner's attention, the commoner cried, "Tell me, sir knight, what does that monk say? Will the abbot come?

"But he must come," Waddard continued, offering Faucon no time to answer. "No matter what my neighbors felt about Dickie, no one should be allowed to desecrate his body this way, not when there's no proof that he, too, will walk."

"Will walk? What reason is there to cut up a corpse that hasn't walked?" Faucon retorted, his voice knife-edged. Either a corpse walked, or it didn't.

Waddard jerked at the harsh reply. His gaze shifted from armed knight to armed knight to armed soldier, then he nervously tucked a strand of sandy-brown hair back under his white cap. And said nothing.

Faucon damned his carelessness and tried again, speaking more gently. "If the villagers haven't witnessed your son's corpse moving, why do they wish to dismember it?"

The commoner shook his head. Fear yet twisted his expression. His lips began to quiver. He scrubbed his hand over his face as if to hide his reaction.

Faucon tried one more time with the question he should have asked first. "How long has your son been dead?"

Lowering his hand from his face, Waddard aimed his gaze at his horse's ears. "We found him this morn, sir," he replied quietly, his words trembling along with his lips.

Then the man gulped in a shaken breath and raised his gaze to his Crowner. "It was his father! His father finally stole him from me!"

"But you said you are the boy's father," Faucon protested, again speaking more harshly than he intended. This man's sentences were as confusing as the garbled utterances of his priest.

This time when Waddard jerked in reaction, his ancient nag snorted and sidled. The beast collided with one side of the deep path then freed a more panicked snort. As it started to back up in the track, Father Godin turned to catch the horse by the bridle. Holding it where it stood, the priest patted Waddard's left leg and spoke to his parishioner, his words too quiet for Faucon to hear. Waddard nodded and again met his Crowner's gaze.

"I am Dickie's father," he said on a watery sigh. "I have been his father since he was three and I threw my cloak over him on the day I wed his mother. He is my only son. Mary save me, I cannot believe he's gone! "But we all knew it would happen, didn't we, Father?" Waddard moaned, looking at his priest.

Tears again trickled down his cheeks. A few caught in his sparse, graying beard and glistened in the sunlight. "Everyone knew what would happen when Raymond returned this year to fulfill his curse. He came to steal Dickie from me and that's what he has at last done."

With that, Waddard turned his head to the side and sobbed in earnest. The priest again patted the man's leg, then the Northerner turned his pale gaze on Faucon. His Adam's apple moved as he struggled to spit out words.

"Dickie wast," his voice strained with his effort, "morthered af hans— wast kilt by his own laten—"

Father Godin drew a deep breath and tried again. "Dickie was kilt by his own dead fader. His fader walks."

"What?!" Alf blurted out this time. Revulsion filled the soldier's face and voice. "Did I understand you rightly? The boy's dead father rose from the grave to kill his own son?"

"Aye, dat is it," the priest replied, offering the soldier a decisive and grateful nod. This time his words were perfectly clear albeit heavily accented.

"Now all my neighbors believe that Dickie will also walk," Waddard moaned. "They want to cut him up to prevent him from doing so, not caring that if they mutilate him this way, doing so for no proven reason, they may cheat him of his home in heaven."

"Sir, what are they saying?" Edmund prompted.

"Say no more for a moment, if you please," Faucon requested of the Englishmen, not wanting to miss a word while he translated for his clerk.

To Edmund he said, "The priest is Father Godin, from a village called Mancetter. The mounted man is the stepfather of a boy who died last night. Both men say that the boy was killed by his dead father, who has been witnessed walking many times. Now the others in their village want to dismember the boy, believing foolishly that he will walk simply because his father does."

"Hardly foolish," Brother Edmund replied, brows raised. "More likely a wise precaution."

"What?!" Faucon cried, again shocked to his core. "Are you saying the boy's dead body will walk simply because his father is a walker?"

"No, I'm saying that the boy may walk because he died after interacting with a walking corpse," Edmund corrected. "Sir, my question isn't yet answered. We must know how many in the village this monstrosity may have affected. Knowing the circumstances of the boy's death will help us determine that."

"What do you mean 'how many?'" Faucon replied, as confusion threatened to make his thoughts spin again. "Only the boy is dead."

"Ah, but these foul creatures often bring the disease of the grave with them," his clerk replied. "Any living soul who is visited by a walker may become infected by this noxious ailment. Those who fall ill swiftly wither and die. Although it doesn't often happen, the newly-dead will sometimes pass that illness onto those who prepare their body for burial. So, how did the boy die? Was it illness or violence?"

"Violence?!" Will protested, sounding as shocked and befuddled as Faucon felt. "What violence? The walking dead are naught but bones and mist that come to suck out a man's soul, which they then feed to their evil master. What violence can they do?"

Faucon's clerk frowned at the knight. "Mist and bones? Why would you think that? Walkers are the corpses of those who once lived, and are thus made of rotting flesh and, yes, bone. But you're right to say they seek to steal men's souls. As for committing violence, a number of Master Walter's tales tell of folk who battled hand-to-hand with the dead, whether the soldiers in Harlequin's army or their own dead kin or neighbors that they discover walking.

"Sir," Edmund continued, now shifting to address Faucon, "if the dead boy fought physically with the walker, he is far more likely to walk. You must determine the manner of his death."

"You're serious?!" Faucon cried, his stomach twisting at the thought of grappling with a reanimated corpse. "These walkers have the strength to physically attack a living man?"

"That is what the tales tell us," his clerk assured him.

Swallowing his gorge, Faucon shifted back to the priest and potter. "Father, was it illness or violence that caused the boy's death?" he asked in English.

Once again Father Godin strove to bring forth words. A moment later he shook his head in defeat and tapped Waddard's left leg. "Waddard, calm de selif, and spaak. Say ja how Dickie die."

Wiping his nose on his sleeve, Waddard brought his watery gaze back to the warriors and monk in front of him. "He was sitting in the smithy when we found him, just after dawn this morning. He was already cold and stiff." His mouth opened as if he meant to say more. Instead, a heart-wrenching moan escaped him. He buried his face in his palms.

Father Godin made an irritable sound and spoke over the grieving father. "Dickie's head is breaked."

As he said this, he lifted a fist and tapped at the top of his head in demonstration. There was no need for his example. His words were clear enough this time.

"Wait again," Faucon once more warned the priest so he could address Brother Edmund. "He says the dead man broke the boy's skull. Are the dead as strong as that? Can they kill in this manner?"

Brother Edmund's brow creased in consideration, then he gave a slow shake of his head. "There's no specific mention of anyone being pummeled in Master Walter's tales. Instead, most usually the victim's arm is grasped by the dead who then seek to drag the living person away from all safety.

"However, consider this, sir," the monk continued. "We

only know what we do of the walking dead because those who tell these tales survived their encounters. But what of those who did not survive? If they died, could we not say that perhaps the dead in this instance did more than merely pull, that they might have killed using brute force?" Again, Edmund's tone was impossibly reasonable, when what he said was anything but.

"Holy Mother of God," Will muttered again, once more crossing himself. This time Alf did the same.

Faucon shook his head slowly, trying to take in the soul-searing notion of battling hand-to-hand with an animated and rotting corpse. Then, deep below his horror, the huntsman in him stirred. However perverse, however terrifying the urge, that part of him longed to track down this odious creature just to see it for himself.

No, he wanted to do more than that. Mad it might be, but he wanted to try his strength against this abomination. He wanted to run it to ground, cut it into pieces, and put it back in its grave where it belonged.

"Did anyone witness your son's dead father as he did this deed?" Faucon asked of Waddard, who was again scrubbing at his face with a sleeve.

"Nay," Waddard said. "There was no one out and about at that time. Instead, Raymond lured Dickie away from the safety of our home long after all of Mancetter was at their nightly rest. Our reeve Aldo declared that it must have been Raymond who'd done murder. Everyone in the village agrees with him," Waddard continued. "Haven't we all witnessed Raymond walking past our doorways? Moreover, before he died, Raymond cursed my wife, vowing that if she dared to wed, he'd kill her and their son. And that he now has surely done.

"Tell them, Father Godin," the potter cried, looking down at his priest. "Tell them about how bold Raymond is, how he often visits you at our church."

"Ja, I seen him," the priest confirmed, his pronunciation growing clearer with every word. "Each time I seen him I kneel and shout the holy words. He goes." As he said that Father Godin made a gesture with his fingers. The motion seemed to indicate that the walker evaporated rather than departed on foot.

"But this last year, Dickie saw him most of all," Waddard added. "Save for the dead, who would have been out of doors last night, away from all safety on a moonless night?"

"Dickie was," Faucon replied, cocking a brow.

"Not by choice." Again, Waddard's eyes glistened. He blinked away his tears. "Dickie said that when his father calls— called to him, he could not resist. Even though he fought with all his will, he had no choice but to go where Raymond bade."

"So this morning, when you found your son dead, no one raised the hue and cry?" Faucon pressed.

"Why?" Waddard asked in surprise. "To chase a corpse that had already returned to its grave?"

Faucon considered the two men for a moment, then looked at his clerk. "Tell me, Brother Edmund," he said in French. "Which seems more likely to you? That a dead man's corpse sought out his living son to kill him, or that a living man committed murder and now seeks to use a dead man to conceal his sin?"

Edmund blinked in surprise at this. "Either are possible, but why do you ask me this, sir? I believe it's yours to determine."

A slow smile bent Faucon's lips. And thus would begin the strangest hunt of his life. "So it is, and so I shall do."

With that, he once more addressed the two men from Mancetter. "It's good that you came to the abbey seeking aid, but it's not the abbot you need. I am Sir Faucon de Ramis, your shire's newly-elected Keeper of the Pleas. As of Michaelmas past, and by the king's command, I, and not our sheriff, now investigate all unnatural deaths in this shire, and only I can call the jury of the hundred for an inquest. As part of my duties, I am also commanded to protect the remains of the murdered until I determine who or what committed the heinous act." Be that murderer alive or dead. "Lead me to Mancetter and I will prevent your neighbors from dismembering Dickie."

As Waddard turned his slow-moving nag and started back up the hillside for the abbey— Father Godin following on foot, Edmund, Alf, and Will walking with the priest to prepare their waiting mounts for departure— Faucon went to speak to the Cistercians and their abbot. Abbot Henry yet stood where he'd stopped, his crucifix yet clutched in his hand. All eleven of his flock now knelt outside the track on the softer verge. Their chanting ceased as Faucon approached their father.

"Sir Faucon? What do these men tell you?" the abbot asked, life returning to his face. He dropped his hand from his wooden cross.

"Before I answer you, tell me this, if you will, my lord," Faucon replied. "Have you heard tales of the dead walking in these parts? And if you have, have you heard that these reanimated corpses use physical force to do murder?"

The kneeling monks moaned and shifted at this.

"May all the saints preserve us!" Abbot Henry cried in horror. "Is that what these two claim?"

Then the Churchman bowed his head and drew a steadying breath. When he again looked at Faucon, all his fear was gone. Instead, his jaw was tight and his eyes had narrowed. He had the look of a warrior ready to draw his sword.

"Pray, Sir Faucon," he commanded. "Pray with all your heart that these two are wrong. Such an occurrence would be a sure sign of the Devil's rising influence in our land."

"My lord, I shall do better than pray," Faucon assured him. "I intend to discover the truth of this boy's death. If I find that there is a corpse which did rise to kill its living son, I vow to you I will hunt down this unnatural creature. Once I have it under my heel, I will dismember it."

As Faucon made this promise, his squeamishness disappeared, consumed by an almost wild excitement over his forthcoming hunt. "When I have done that, perhaps you, and any other Churchmen you need, will help me to put those pieces back into his grave to make certain that he never again strays."

"That I can do," the abbot replied with a nod. "Go you, and begin your hunt. In the meanwhile, I'll send word to Canterbury, or perhaps Hereford, since there's no bishop at Coventry just now. The Evil One must not be allowed to work his wiles unchecked here in Arden. Or anywhere else in our world," he added softly before continuing.

"Now, as to your question of folk who may have seen the dead afoot here. There are many who claim they have, but I don't believe that all have seen what they claim. I think most simply repeat the tales crafted to frighten them and their children into staying within the safety of their village or town walls at night."

That made sense to Faucon. This had surely been the purpose of his mother's stories of Harlequin. She'd used them like chains, seeking to imprison her young and too-boisterous sons on their pallets at night. It had worked, at least until the time came that her boys were fostered out of her home and care.

"But there are others whose stories have the ring of truth to them," the abbot was saying. "I've heard enough folk speak of seeing the army of that ancient king marching on the Street that I must believe this is a regular occurrence. As for a dead man battling physically with the living—"

Henry of Merevale shuddered and shook his head. "That is something I have never heard. Frankly, it's something I pray you prove to be untrue and that I never again hear."

With that, the abbot turned to face his flock. "Brothers, up with you all. Save your fears and your prayers for later, when we can kneel together in our own chapel. Our day is far from finished. Those of you who have work to complete before our repast, best get to it. Brother Augustine, take whomever you need to help you in the kitchen."

The tall monk nodded. "Father, I believe I may need a few additional fish for the stew," he said, then shot a look in Faucon's direction as if to remind the abbot of his earlier invitation to their guests.

"A good idea," Abbot Henry replied. "Return to the kitchen ahead of me. I'll be along with what you need in a bit."

As the monks dispersed, Faucon offered the abbot a warm smile. "I would thank you again for your offer of hospitality, my lord. Given what lies ahead, I cannot say if we'll be able to accept. Please do not delay your meal for us."

"And given what's occurred, I cannot say I expected anything else," the abbot replied with a friendly nod. "However, my offer stands. Mancetter isn't far, only a short walk by foot, or at least by my feet. I've visited the place several times to meet the wool buyer who purchases our fleece. What with your party all riding, you'll make short work of the distance.

"Know that should you decide to return for the night, you are welcome at any hour. Just knock on our gate. I'll promote Brother Samuel to porter for the night. We've no gatehouse but he never minds sleeping on the ground under the stars. Just be sure to knock loudly." Once again Henry of Merevale winked. "Brother Samuel sleeps soundly no matter where he lays his head."

With that Faucon's unsettled thoughts finally came to rest. He laughed. "Then I hope it is I and not the walking dead who disturbs the monk's rest later this evening, my lord abbot."

"As do we all," the Churchman assured him with yet another shudder. "I've changed my mind, Sir Faucon. I'm very grateful that I called for you to come. Had I not, I would be going to Mancetter in your stead, and after listening to you, I think I am wholly unprepared for such a task, while you are not.

"Now be off with you. But as you go, give me your vow that you'll return here to me before you depart our vale. Regardless of what occurs, you must share what you discover, in case there is anything I must convey to those who better understand these matters."

"I so vow," Faucon replied. "If you will, my lord, pray for us. Bid our Lord and all His saints to guide me and mine in this hunt."

"So I and all my brothers will do," the Churchman replied.

Faucon expected the abbot to present his ring for the ritual kiss. Instead, Henry of Merevale offered his hand the way that knights did. Surprised and pleased, Faucon closed his fingers around the Churchman's palm.

"May our Lord bless and keep you," the abbot said, then freed his hand to make the sign of the cross. "And God speed," he added, before starting back toward the fish ponds.

Chapter Three

Faucon trailed Brother Augustine and two other monks up the track. At the crest of the hill, the abbey's wooden exterior wall rose up before him. Father Godin and Waddard— the commoner yet astride his nag while the priest once again held the horse's bridle— waited near the only opening in that protective wall. The two commoners watched without comment as Faucon strode past them to enter the courtyard through the narrow arched gateway.

Once inside the wall, Faucon again glanced around him in approval. Unlike other holy houses that were busily rebuilding in stone and slate, Merevale made do with humble wooden structures and thatched roofs. The small church, a large kitchen, and single long house raised on a stone foundation that served the monks as their chapter house, frater, dorter, abbot's office, and cellar, were most likely the same buildings the brothers had raised upon the founding of their home. Again, the unpretentious simplicity spoke to him.

There were other structures in the compound, but these were the sort found on any self-sustaining farmstead— a threshing barn, two hay sheds, and a very large sheep-fold. Lining the fold were a number of lean-tos, no doubt where the brothers stored their shearing tools along with shorn fleece. Beyond the sheep-fold was Brother Augustine's pear orchard and a small paddock where Faucon and his party had left their mounts to graze.

All three men were already mounted. Alf and Will turned their horses in Faucon's direction, Will leading Legate, while

Brother Edmund did his best to goad his donkey into movement. Even from where Faucon stood it was clear the stubborn little beast was equally determined to resist, having decided to stay the night with the monks.

His helmet once more in place, Alf offered his employer a nod as he rode past, heading for the gate. Will halted his courser near Faucon and tossed his younger brother Legate's reins. As Faucon rose into his saddle, he shot a look heavenward.

Now that Christmas was but a few weeks away, the days had grown short. At best they had no more than an hour of light left to the day. If Mancetter was as close as the abbot said, that was likely time enough to claim the boy's body in the king's name. But that wasn't all that needed doing. He had to find a secure place to store the corpse for the night. If that took even the slightest amount of time, night would fall before they could start back for the abbey.

And what if there were no secure place for the body in Mancetter? Well then, the four of them would be staying in the village for the night, to guard the boy's remains.

That wasn't a welcome thought, not if Brother Edmund was right about the possibility of the boy walking after death. What if they needed to bind Dickie's body? The thought of watching a corpse struggling to free itself made Faucon's stomach twist again.

"Gauging the time, are you?" Will asked with a laugh when Faucon brought his gaze back to his brother. "So tell me. How far are we from this unholy place where a dead father rises from the grave to kill his living son? I'm not certain how I feel about riding in the dark across a land where the dead walk and Harlequin rides."

Faucon smiled at that. "I couldn't agree more. The abbot assures me the village isn't far. Best you pray, brother. Pray that all goes well and swiftly so we can return here to these walls before full dark and enjoy that perry."

"That I shall do," Will replied on a not-quite-amused

breath.

Then he sent Faucon a laughing sidelong look. "Or perhaps I won't. I wonder what it's like, watching a corpse walk? What say you? Shall we sit up all the night long and find out for ourselves?" In that moment Will sounded like the older brother Faucon had once adored, the one who had never refused a challenge, and had never sought to hurt his younger sibling for no reason.

"I will if you will," Faucon shot back with a grin.

That had Will laughing again. "If we must, we shall."

Just then Brother Edmund's donkey streaked past them at almost a gallop. The monk had his arms wrapped around the creature's neck. Although the long basket that contained Edmund's scribbling tools was safely strapped to his back, it bounced wildly.

Faucon sucked in a worried breath. It would be one thing if his clerk fell, but if that basket spilled, they'd be delayed well past nightfall as Edmund collected and reorganized his belongings. He kicked Legate into motion.

"I'm coming for you," he shouted after the monk.

His rescue attempt proved unnecessary. By the time Legate exited through the abbey's gateway, Father Godin had caught Edmund's little mount. That the donkey had given up any resistance and stood calmly, only his ears twitching, said the Northern priest had more than a little familiarity with horses and their kin.

As for Edmund he remained bent over the neck of his despised mount, his basket blessedly intact. Panting, eyes closed, he came slowly upright. Faucon grinned again. Edmund's inability to master his little beast was proof that a university education wasn't the only training a man— even a Churchman— needed to make his way in life.

"Waddard," Faucon said, looking at the potter on his bony nag, "your horse is the slowest. You'll ride ahead of us to set the pace.

"Alf?" Faucon turned toward the English soldier and

shifted into French for the sake of Will and Edmund. "Take Mancetter's priest up with you and ride at the back. Brother Edmund, you'll ride in front of Alf. Will, you'll ride between me and my clerk."

Much to Faucon's surprise, Father Godin released the donkey's bridle and started toward Alf without waiting for a translation. If the priest spoke French, why hadn't he used that language to communicate with Brother Samuel? Then again, perhaps he had, only to discover his accent made him indecipherable in two languages.

Ahead of him, Waddard urged his mount onto what looked like a footpath. Unlike the steep side of the abbey's hill, which was planted with fruit and nut trees, this side, the one with the gentler incline, had been left a grassy, shrubby waste. That made it useful for nothing save fodder for sheep.

At the bottom of the hill, their path intersected with another track, this one a good deal wider and often used, or so said the pair of well-worn ruts that cut into its face. Judging by their depth and spacing, heavily-laden wagons— the sort that would carry both that buyer of wool the abbot mentioned and all the fleece that man came to purchase— often traveled along here.

They had barely turned upon this pathway when tall, dry grasses and shrubs gave way abruptly to a dense copse. Here, the trees were so large that Faucon judged them ancient. It was a reminder of what the Forest of Arden had been in some long-ago age. Unlike Feckenham, Arden had not been claimed by England's first Norman king. Instead, it had been carved into pieces— including the piece that would one day come to Faucon— this virgate belonging to that knight's manor, those hides owned by some baron's estate, or by some monastery. With no one overseer, each landholder did as he wished, whether that was to harvest every last one of the great trees— oak, hazelnut, and linden, to feed his fire, build his manor, or make charcoal to temper his iron— or to leave the land wild to attract the beasts of the hunt.

This was one of the wild slices. Indeed, the tangled canopy overhead was so thick and wide-spread that little light penetrated, even now that every branch was bare. A daunted sun hadn't prevented brilliant green moss and airy ferns from growing up around each massive trunk. Where light did reach the soil, stands of glossy holly, or sloe and elderberry— presently just winter skeletons— had taken root. With those creatures that slept through the cold now abed and the chittering birds and waterfowl gone for the season, it was as hushed in here as a monastery at midnight. Not even their horses' hooves sounded, what with a thick layer of damp leaf litter covering the ground. Instead, Legate's every step stirred up the sweet spice of autumnal decay.

Just then, Will brought his courser alongside Legate. "Beware! Here is the place where the dead walk and you must one day live," he taunted, his overly-loud voice shattering both the stillness and Faucon's moment of peace. There was a harsh, envious edge to his words. That was a sure sign that not-Will had returned.

Faucon smiled to hide how deeply he disliked this facsimile of his brother. "I'm doomed."

"And always have been, so say I," not-Will retorted with an unkind laugh.

To respond was to encourage further conversation with the unnatural creature who was not his brother. Thus, Faucon kept his gaze on the track and rode on in silence. Not-Will retreated only when the trees gave way again to grassland.

The man who owned this next piece of Arden had chosen to harvest all the hardwoods, but had left their stumps to use for coppicing. Thus had once proud oaks and ash been humbled into large bushes, each one sporting a dozen or more straight, slender branches destined to become handles for tools or the supports for a thatched roof. When the track curved, the stunted trees disappeared behind a thick hedgerow. On this side of the living fence, every leaf and smaller twig was gone almost to the height of Legate's shoulder eaten by wild browsers.

Curious what lay beyond the hedge, Faucon stood in his stirrups. It was as he expected, fields and orchards, each outlined with their own protective hedgerows. In the distance was a thick, square stone church tower. Perhaps two dozen gentle reedy mounds clustered near the church tower, most emitting lines of twining, curling smoke— thatched-roofed homes.

That had Faucon once again glancing at the sun, only to note how much closer it was to the horizon. He urged Legate forward until he rode next to Waddard. "Is this Mancetter?" he asked hopefully.

"Nay, Atherstone," the commoner replied without looking at his Crowner, once again using his sleeve to wipe away his grief. "Atherstone is but a spit of a place, not at all like Mancetter." Although his voice was filled with pride and scorn, his tone sounded more like bluster, meant to disguise his raw emotions.

"Will we reach Watling Street on this track?" Faucon asked, this time out of simple curiosity.

"We would if we were going that far." Waddard kept his gaze trained on a spot between his horse's ears. "But Mancetter isn't quite on the Street, what with the River Anker between us and it. You'll see.

"Oh, and by the bye," the commoner continued, still speaking to his horse's head, "I doubt you knights will think there's a place in Mancetter suitable for you to lay your heads. Given the hour, sir, once we arrive, perhaps you should send your clerk or your man to the manor. They should ask the monks if there's room for you to board with them for the night. The manor isn't far from our church."

Once again, although Faucon completely understood what Waddard said, the man's words confused him. Monks lived in convents, not manors. "Do you mean your lord?" he asked to clarify, in case grief had addled Waddard more than Faucon already knew.

The commoner shot his Crowner a watery sidelong glance. He shook his head. "We no longer have a lord. He gave our village and all these lands to some abbey in Normandy. They then sent monks to live in the old manor house, where we still go to make our payments.

"They're a strange bunch, these monks, almost hermits some of them. Maybe that's why the abbey sent them to a strange land, so it would be easier for them to keep to themselves. For certain that's why Father Godin and I flew to Merevale rather than the manor. There's never any help for us from those monks, not for anyone from Mancetter.

"Do you see that?" Waddard pointed back to the sliver of the stone church tower they could now see over the top of the hedgerow. "The monks spent what we in Mancetter gave them to build a big church for Atherstone and its few souls, when all we have is a small, wooden church. Wouldn't we like a fine, stone church as well?" he complained. "I mean, are we not as worthy as our neighbors? And aren't there more of us in Mancetter than Atherstone? After all, our village is the head of the parish!"

His ire spent, Waddard fell into an abrupt silence, once again studying his horse's head. Much to Faucon's surprise, a moment later the commoner added, "Then again, if the monks built us a church, that'd be the end of Father Godin." His voice was low enough that he might have been speaking to himself.

"How so?" Faucon asked, even though polite convention dictated that he should ignore the comment.

The potter shot him a startled glance. For a moment Faucon thought the man might not reply. Then the commoner shrugged.

"Well, Father Godin isn't actually our priest. Father Berold has gone mad." As Waddard said this, he made a number of wild and jerky motions with one hand. "He no longer has the strength to enter our church, not even during the daylight hours, not even to save his own soul, much less ours. When Father Berold could no longer leave his house, didn't we go to the monks to beg for a new priest, it being their right to appoint one for us?" This was an aggrieved comment.

"They heard our pleas but did nothing, and we got no new priest. Those of us who wanted to hear a mass had to crowd in with the monks in that tiny chapel of theirs, or walk to Atherstone, seething with the sin of envy over their fine church. Then almost a year ago Father Godin and his wife came down Watling Street and stopped in Mancetter."

Faucon's brows rose at that. He knew many a clergyman kept himself a convenient housekeeper, but none of them were open about calling her what she was, a wife.

"We warned Father Godin about Raymond, but he said he wasn't afraid. He said his faith was stronger than Father Berold's. Perhaps it is, because his word has proven true. Despite that Raymond reached our church almost every week, that hasn't driven Father Godin from us.

"We told him we couldn't offer him any payment, not when we were still supporting Father Berold, he yet being our true priest and all. Father Godin said he didn't need anything from us. He said he'd use what we gave Father Berold, that it was enough to care for all three of them— himself, his wife and that poor wracked man— for as long as Father Berold might live.

"And so Father Godin and his wife have done," Waddard hastily assured his Crowner. "They're good folk, and very grateful for the sanctuary we gave them. As for us, we were all just thankful to have a priest in our own church again."

Again Waddard fell quiet, only to sigh a moment later. "I suppose the monks already know that we've replaced Father Berold with Father Godin. How could they not know, when we all stopped attending their masses? I suppose someday they'll force Father Godin to move on, it being their right to choose for us. That'll be a sad day for us all."

Faucon shook his head. This affair got stranger with every step. "Leave me to worry over where I and my party spend this coming night. The only thing that matters at the moment is to see your son's body protected before nightfall."

Waddard jerked at the reminder of what he'd lost. His shoulders hunched and he choked a little, as if trying to restrain a sob. Faucon reined Legate back into position behind the nag, giving the man privacy to mourn as he would, and studied the land around him.

The hedgerows had ended, suggesting they'd left Atherstone's fields behind them, and the land was again a shrubby waste. That was, except for an area where Faucon could see new tillage, He frowned. Not tillage, at least it didn't look like any tilling he'd ever seen done by the blade of a plow. Instead the torn earth had the look of foraging hogs to him.

As they neared one of the turned patches, his brows rose in appreciation. And what good work those hogs had done! Great clumps of grasses, the sort with roots so thick they stopped the plow blade, had been completely uprooted. So had all the smaller bushes and saplings. The owner of this plot need only rake off the debris then bring in oxen and a plow to cut in new rows. Now, why hadn't he or his father thought of using their hogs to clear their wasteland?

Just then the breeze lifted. Caught in its folds were chill hints of the oncoming night and the rich, moist scent of river water. "And now, sir, we have reached Mancetter," Waddard announced without looking back at his Crowner.

Chapter Four

A head of them stood a pair of wattle-and-daub homes, one on either side of the path. Each cottage stood so close to the track that Faucon could have touched the edges of their thatched roofs if he'd stretched out his arms. That cheated the householders of their toft— the space used for a front garden— although both homes did have a few herbs planted along their front walls. Ah, but what these owners gave up in front, they regained behind their homes. The line of withe fencing behind each house suggested a surprisingly generous croft, the area where a family kept their own livestock and gardens.

Beyond that first pair of homes was another pair, also set up against the road and enclosed in withe fencing. The leftward house had suffered damage and had been temporarily patched with a withe panel. After that was yet another similar pair, then another, and another. The pattern repeated for as far as Faucon could see, which was to the roof line of the wooden church that Waddard despised and Raymond haunted. Unlike some villages that clustered around their church and green, Mancetter was long and narrow, and snaked along with the track that cut it in twain.

In an instant the village dogs appeared in the track in front of Waddard. Although they barked viciously, the curs kept to the verge until all the horses, with their iron-shod hooves, passed. Then, yet offering toothless snarls and impotent growls, they reentered the track to follow.

The dogs weren't the only creatures in Mancetter to take notice of the travelers. Offering irritated squawks, chickens fled the path. Someone's flock of geese honked out the alarm. A spotted sow stretched out in front of her owner's house, her head pillowed on the doorstep, opened her eye to study Faucon as he rode past.

From both in front of and behind them, leather hinges creaked. Doors opened. Men, some wearing only their shirts and chausses, others with leather aprons over their tunics, stepped outside to warily eye the armed men in their track. Housewives, babes in arms and shawls over their shoulders, stained linen overgowns atop their brightly-colored gowns, stopped behind their menfolk. Younger children clung to their mothers' skirts, staring wide-eyed, while their older, braver siblings dared each other to touch the knights as they rode past.

At first Faucon wondered if the threat of a murdering corpse had driven the village folk inside for the day. Then he remembered that this was the season when all rural folk retreated inside their own walls. With the spring wheat planted and manure spread on those fields that would sleep until Candlemas, there were no more communal chores left in the year. That gave each family two months to work for themselves, be that spinning wool into thread, weaving fabric, making garments, crafting tools, clearing a new garden, or building another shed.

One thing was certain. Waddard was right to claim that every soul in his village had seen Raymond walk. Here in Mancetter, no traveler, dead or alive, would ever pass unnoticed.

When they were only three pairs of homes away from the low wooden wall encircling Mancetter's churchyard, a petite housewife stepped to the center of the track. She looked worn to the bone, her face haggard, her skin ashen, and dark smudges beneath her eyes. Like all married women, common or noble, her head was modestly covered with a linen headcloth, but a few fine strands of fair hair had escaped to straggle around her thin face. The sleeves of her blue gown were rolled up above her elbows. When she crossed her arms, Faucon saw the same crusting reddish dirt that fouled her sleeveless linen overgown marked her hands and forearms.

"Juliana?" Waddard called to her in surprise. "What are you doing?"

"Why Husband, I am looking behind you for the abbot you went to fetch," Waddard's wife replied sarcastically. "Where is the Churchman we so need, and who are these knights riding with you?"

As the potter's wife spoke three tiny girls slipped out of her doorway. The youngest— naught but a toddler— clung to the next tallest girl, while the middle lass clutched her older sister's arm. All of them wore gowns of pretty green, and all had hair so fair that it looked almost white, even in the fading light. Although they were petite like their mother, and had her narrow face, time and life had yet to pinch their features as it had hers.

Two older lasses, the eldest surely no more than twelve, their hair the color of honey, followed their younger siblings. Although they wore gowns of the same pale blue as their mother, it was Waddard's reflection and his grief that Faucon saw in their faces. These two were bolder. They came to stand behind their mother in the track.

As Waddard halted his ancient nag before the woman who had once been Raymond's wife, Faucon raised a hand, signaling his party to halt. Edmund wasn't quick enough with his reins. His donkey pushed forward, stopping only when he was between Legate and the verge. That trapped the monk's foot against the side of the track. Muttering in irritation, he yanked it free, then dismounted to stand on the verge.

"Juliana, I bring someone even more powerful than the abbot," the potter told his wife. His voice was tense, suggesting long-running discord between them. At his call the door to the cottage closest to the churchyard fence opened, and an old woman leaned out to look up the track at her neighbors.

"This is Sir Faucon de Ramis, our shire's new Keeper of the Pleas," Waddard was saying. "By the order of our king it is he, rather than our sheriff, who now investigates all unnatural deaths and calls our jury. Sir Faucon says the king has also given him the power to protect Dickie's body. This he has promised to do. He will keep Dickie safe until he calls the jury to accuse Raymond of killing our son."

Faucon frowned at Waddard's misunderstanding of his duties. But as his mouth opened to correct him, a man's frantic shout echoed forward from the roadway behind them. "These knights come to protect Dickie's corpse?! What of us? Who will protect us from Dickie?"

Turning in his saddle, Faucon looked back along the track. The dogs had dispersed. In their place was a gaggle of youths, no boy among them old enough to sport more than a wisp of a beard. Standing with them was a lass wearing dark blue. She was a pretty thing, with fine features set in an oval face and thick black hair. Her wide-set dark eyes were reddened and the downward pull of her full lips suggested grief.

As the lass caught him looking at her, she bowed her head and swiftly stepped up onto the verge. Darting around Brother Edmund, she moved off in the direction of the church. The youths milled for an instant, glancing between each other, then followed her. The old woman crossed her arms as the young-sters passed in front of her home on their way to the church-yard.

The departure of the youths left about four dozen adults yet in the roadway. Although they were mostly men, a surpris-ing number of women stood among them. Given that he'd tallied over sixty homes since that first pair of cottages, it seemed that most of Mancetter's householders had joined this procession.

"Milo is right, Waddard," shouted a heavy-set man wearing a blanket over his shirt and chausses. "We all know how much trouble Dickie was while alive." He paused to glance around at his neighbors. "We all agree he's sure to be just as much trouble in death, isn't he?"

"Like father, like son," agreed an oldster. He held a ragged cloak closed around him with one hand as he shook his finger at the potter. "Waddard, you went to Merevale on a fool's errand. Even if you'd brought the abbot with you, neither he nor these knights can stop us. Admit it. You know we're right, and so is what we mean to do."

"Tell us, sirs. How do you intend to protect us from a corpse we all know will walk?" called yet another man, his powerful voice radiating forward from the back of the crowd.

As his challenge reverberated off the houses at either side of the track, folk began to shuffle and shift, opening a way for him. In his middle years, he was tall and broad-shouldered. Unlike the others, he wore no cloak or blanket to protect him from the onset of a chill evening. Fair hair hung to his shoulders, framing his square-jawed face. A thick scar, one that suggested a blade, ran from beneath his left eye to his jaw. It had cut deeply enough to leave a bare patch through his thick golden-red beard. If this man had once been a soldier, whatever his present occupation, it kept him just as fit. His green tunic stretched taut over his upper arms and hung loosely across his belly.

Faucon shifted toward Waddard. "This is your reeve?" he asked in a low voice. In truth, he needed no one to tell him that this was the man who ruled Mancetter; both his challenge and his swagger said as much.

Waddard, already twisted in his saddle as far as pain would allow, nodded. "Aldo is also our smith," he offered, his voice equally as low and his tone cautious. "It was in his smithy that we found Dickie this morn."

"Aldo, leave be," Father Godin called as he slid off the back of Alf's horse. Coming to earth without stumbling, he turned to face his flock, his fist on his hips. "Dis ist a ting for our Church and the king's man, not any a ja. Go to home, all a ja."

"What right have you to instruct us?" the reeve shot back as he came to a stop at the front of the crowd, just out of arm's reach of the priest. "It's you who will no longer have a place here if you persist in protecting one who doesn't deserve your protection. Nor can you expect us to sit idly by and do nothing, not when we all know what will happen. If there's naught we can do to stop Raymond, we can stop Dickie. All of us, even you, Father, know what must be done."

He half-turned to glance at those behind him. "Do we not?" The folk he ruled supported him with a roar of approval.

"Why do we listen to this Churchman? He's not even our priest," a woman shouted angrily. "Father Berold would never have stolen Dickie's body from us. Nor would he have locked us out of our own church."

Faucon found her easily in the crowd. Her brown gown clung to her voluptuous form. Her resemblance to the pretty girl said that, if they were not mother and daughter, they were surely kin. Unlike modest wives who pulled their head coverings to the top of their foreheads to conceal their hair, this woman wore hers pushed back to the middle of her head. Thick wings of black hair swooped out from under her scarf, falling softly over her cheekbones and framing a face that would have been lovely if it hadn't been twisted in anger.

She pushed her way forward until she stood next to her reeve, then turned to face those behind her. "Neighbors, we should drive this imposter priest from Mancetter and do it this very moment. He should be punished for his daring!"

When only a few in the crowd lifted their voices in agreement, she pressed her case. "Hear me, all of you! Alive, that boy took my daughter, ruining her. Now that he's dead, I won't have him seducing my Tibby into following him!" That won a much stronger reaction from those watching, albeit more surprise than outrage.

"My son did no rape to Tibby!" Juliana cried in protest.

Trapped in front of her husband's nag, she shifted right then left, but could find no safe pathway through the horses. Unable to confront her son's accuser, she settled for shrieking, "If Tibby says Dickie took her against her will, she's as much of a lightskirt as you are, Bett."

"How dare you!" Bett shouted in the direction of the potter's wife.

"Juliana, mind your tongue!" Waddard shouted at the same instant. From atop his mount, he extended a forestalling hand. "Now is not the time for this."

Raymond's former wife turned her blazing gaze on her second husband. Her mouth trembled. "Now is not the time," she mocked, her voice raised to a level that all but the most distant in the crowd could hear her. "That's what you said three days ago when I warned you what would happen if you did not allow me to act. Nor was it 'the time' the day before that, nor the day before that. Now, there's no time left, all because you refused to take even the smallest action at any time to stop this!"

Waddard blanched. "Juliana!" He turned his wife's name into a shocked cry.

Flinching, he wrenched around in his saddle to plead with his reeve. "Aldo, I pray you take no heed of my wife. She is bereft and doesn't know what she's saying."

"I know exactly what I am saying," Juliana retorted. "I've never known better what I must say than in this moment. I'm saying that if anyone is to blame for Dickie's death, it is you, Waddard." As she spoke, she yanked off her head covering and threw it to the ground, then pulled at her overgown as if she meant to undress in front of everyone.

"Mama, stop!" her eldest daughter cried in shock. Beside her, her next younger sister snatched up the discarded head-cloth and hugged it to her chest. Her eyes wide, she glanced between her parents.

Juliana ignored her children. "Listen closely, all of you," she shouted again to her neighbors, yet yanking at her over-gown. "Hear me as I say that if Tibby is ruined, it's because she wanted Dickie to ruin her. I'm saying that each and every one of you who dares to celebrate my son's death today are the very cause of his demise. Rather than help me, all you wanted to do was blame him for Raymond's wrongs, when my child never knew his sire.

"Now, today when you should know guilt, you instead harden your hearts and seek to deny my child, my precious son, any chance at heaven! Should you succeed, know that I will forever pray that all of you are damned for what you wish to do to him!"

Her curse reverberated off the houses on either side of her and sent shock rippling over the crowd. At the same instant Juliana's overgown tore down the middle. She shrugged it off her shoulders. When it lay in the roadway, she gave it a vicious kick and looked at her husband.

"All the years I've wasted! Would that I had never wed with you!" she screeched, then lifted her skirts and raced in the direction of the church.

"Mama!" her next oldest daughter protested, her voice breaking in pain as all her sisters began to cry.

"Juliana, come back!" Waddard called after her, sounding heartsick.

Chapter Five

Faucon breathed out in disappointment as he watched the potter's wife run. Oncoming night had painted the whitewashed homes around him a gentle gray, and dark shadows now piled softly in every corner. There'd be no perry for them tonight. Instead, they'd make their beds on the hard floor of Mancetter's church alongside a dead boy who might seek to escape them at any moment.

The old woman in the cottage nearest the church still stood in her doorway. After Juliana raced past her, she retreated inside her walls, leaving her door wide. At the churchyard fence, Dickie's mother scrambled out of the track and dashed through the gate that Tibby and that gaggle of youths must have left open behind them.

As his wife raced across the grassy yard toward the church door, Waddard yanked painfully around on his nag to address his reeve. "You must forgive her, Aldo," he cried frantically. "Neighbors, you all must forgive her. You know Juliana. You've known her all her life. Has she ever before behaved like this? Nay, she has not. She's crazed with grief."

"I do not forgive her," Bett shouted. "Aldo, I demand you fine Waddard for the slander his wife spews at me."

"Dismount," Faucon told Will and Alf at the same time, his voice low enough to keep his words between them. "We're for the church."

Then he looked at his clerk, who yet stood on the verge. "Brother Edmund, hurry ahead of us and stand ready at the church door. You'll enter the instant it opens to guard the boy's body while we hold the door against these folk," he told the monk, when what he really wanted was to keep Brother Edmund out of harm's way.

With a nod the monk lifted his heels into what was almost a trot. That was both unusual compliance and speed for him. As Alf followed Edmund along the verge, Will dismounted. Faucon's brother smirked. "Does our king allow his new Coronarius to kill his subjects? If so, know that I'm willing to help."

Faucon clenched his teeth, biting back his frustration with his brother. Before his accident Will would never have uttered such nonsense. It had been their father's first lesson, given on the day he put wooden swords into their small hands. An honorable man only drew his weapon at the command of his liege lord or his king, or when he had exhausted all other means of resolution. Even an idiot could see how complicated this situation was. Violence would destroy any hope of cooperation, and cooperation was what Faucon craved most from Mancetter's folk, for he was swimming in questions.

Blessedly, Will turned to follow Alf rather than demand a response. Faucon started after his brother, then glanced over his shoulder at Father Godin. "Father, you must open the church for us so we can protect the boy's body," he called in French, hoping he was right about the man's fluency.

He was. The priest whirled. In an instant, the churchman had threaded between the standing horses and passed the yet-mounted Waddard. Then, lifting the skirt of his long gown, he raced full tilt in the direction of his church.

"Our priest means to allow these strangers into our church," Aldo bellowed at the same time, revealing that he also understood the tongue of his betters. "We cannot allow them to keep us from reaching Dickie's corpse. Hie, all of you!"

Mail jangling, Faucon kept pace with Will while ahead of them Alf dogged Brother Edmund's heels. Father Godin darted past the knights, then around the soldier and the monk to dash through the open gateway. Juliana was already on the nave porch. She crouched to one side of the locked door, her head buried against her knees, her shoulders shaking.

Again Faucon glanced behind him, this time looking to see where the reeve was. The smith was only now passing Waddard's horse as the potter struggled to dismount. That had Faucon wondering if what Mancetter's reeve really wanted was a chance to beat his shield in front of a stronger foe, seeking to impress those he ruled.

If that was Aldo's intention, then it was a shame only a few would witness their headman's performance. Only Bett and a dozen men had answered Aldo's call to follow him. The rest of the villagers in the track were putting their backs to their reeve and their church, choosing instead to return to the safety and warmth of their own hearths and homes.

Ahead of Faucon, Will climbed out of the roadway to jog through the gate into the churchyard. Alf and Brother Edmund were almost at the porch steps, while a panting Father Godin now stood before the church door. As the priest pulled a large iron key out of the leather scrip that hung from his rope belt, Juliana came to her feet. Standing with her head bowed, the grieving mother swayed a little.

Faucon eyed the church door as he followed Will across the yard. As with any door built from heavy oak, long metal braces extended from its massive hinges to help support the weight of the wood. But there was another metal strip— one not connected to a hinge— on this door. Nailed above the handle, it aligned with a second metal strap that was fastened to the church wall. A massive iron lock connected the two straps. Thus, was the door held shut without the need of a bar or someone inside to man that bar.

The priest turned the key in the lock, then removed it. With his other hand, he yanked at the lock, then yanked again, then twisted and pulled, seeking to free the shank from the holes in the two straps. Tucking the key back into his scrip, Father Godin then fixed both hands around the lock and pulled with all his might. Juliana eased closer to him.

Metal scraped on metal as the shank came free. The priest

rocked back on his heels. In the same instant, Dickie's mother lunged forward and threw open the door. It slammed into Father Godin. Already off balance, he stumbled backwards, then dropped to sit on the porch floor.

"Of all the insolence!" Brother Edmund shouted at the woman, dashing across the porch to scold. He was too late. Juliana had fled into the church.

"Brother Edmund," Faucon called to his clerk as he followed Will toward the porch steps, "take Father Godin inside now and be quick about it. Alf, open the door to its widest. Will, hie! Join Alf in the doorway. Stand with your swords drawn, tips to the ground."

As monk and priest entered the church, Alf took his assigned position. Will bypassed the steps and leapt onto the porch. He joined the English soldier in the arched opening as Faucon reached the center of the porch. Turning to face the yard, he stood with his arms relaxed at his sides and his sword yet sheathed.

The reeve entered the yard with only Bett and six men at his back, half of his original support. The other six, craven laggards all, had stopped at the corner of the old woman's house. There they huddled in the deepening shadows, all of them watching the churchyard.

Faucon's lip curled. Mancetter's men were no different than their dogs. Like that pack of curs, they were content to slink cautiously along, offering only the pretense of threat.

Aldo came no farther than the porch steps. No surprise that. Had the reeve closed the gap between him and those he pretended to challenge, it would have been an indication that he intended to provoke violence.

As the reeve's remaining male supporters gathered close behind him, Bett continued forward until she stood alongside the big man. "Why do you halt?" she demanded, asking the question that Mancetter's menfolk should have posed. "Lead us to the door. They are only three. We can push past them and enter our church."

Aldo ignored her, his gaze on Faucon. "Who are you to prevent us from entering our own church?" he demanded in English.

Again Faucon's lip curled, this time his scorn aimed at the reeve. For all his size and bulk, Faucon wondered what sort of soldier Aldo had been. As blows went, this one was badly thought out and poorly executed.

"I am Sir Faucon de Ramis, your shire's newly-elected Keeper of the Pleas," he replied in the same tongue. That won a startled blink from the reeve and open surprise from the men behind him. "I am charged with protecting the body of Dickie of Mancetter until the jury of the hundred is called to confirm the name of the one who took his life. Know that to challenge me is to challenge our king."

At his proclamation the men behind Aldo glanced uneasily at each other. Almost as one, they took a backward step. Not so Bett. The pretty woman lifted her head to a proud angle. Her eyes narrowed.

"You're a stranger to us, sir, known here by no man," she said to Faucon. "What proof do you offer that you are who you say and have the rights you proclaim?"

The reeve yelped as the woman's insult struck him instead of the man she'd intended to disparage. And just like that, control of this encounter fell neatly into Faucon's hands. He pulled his sword from its sheath. Resting the tip on the porch floor between his feet, he folded his hands over the pommel.

"You know who I am and the duties our king has laid upon me because you just heard me tell you what they are," Faucon replied coldly to the woman, then looked at Aldo. "What say you, reeve? Do you agree with her? Do you believe that I, the king's servant in this shire, lie in an attempt to play you and the rest of Mancetter false?"

Panic dashed across the reeve's face. He looked at the woman. "Go home, Bett," he commanded too late.

She stared at him, her mouth ajar. "I will not!"

"You will. You and your careless tongue have no place

here," Aldo almost snarled.

When she didn't move, he gave her a sharp push. She stumbled back with a cry. "Go, or I promise you'll be the one I fine for bad behavior."

Shock flattened Bett's expression. Her eyes began to glisten but she held her ground. "You would do that to me?! What of my Tibby? That boy was a rogue in life, just like his father. He'll be a rogue in death, I know it, aye. He'll come for her tonight. You cannot allow him to take Tibby from me."

Aldo crossed his arms and put his shoulder to the woman. Freeing another sharp cry, Bett turned to the men behind him. "What's wrong with all of you? No knight, no matter who he claims to be, nor any abbot, nor bishop, nor even our king can force us to face evil! Nor can anyone promise to protect us against the same, not unless they do to that corpse what must be done!"

Again Faucon bit back a smile as Bett unwittingly battered at her reeve for a second time. Once again, Faucon grabbed the advantage she offered. "Can the men of Mancetter not control their women?" he chided, his tongue honed to a cutting edge. "Reeve, best you make this one understand that I now control what happens to the boy's body. If she or anyone else attempts to desecrate his corpse, death will be the price. If she cannot understand that, then you had better see her confined for her safety."

"Sir, the light is ebbing!" Edmund called from inside the church, his tone urgent. "You must come within this very moment."

Faucon ignored his clerk. Even the smallest distraction might cost him the very thing he'd stolen from Aldo. Much to his surprise, Alf spoke in his stead.

"Our Crowner cannot come, Brother Edmund. The villagers question Sir Faucon's right to claim the body. They worry that he intends to force them to face evil, and that he will not or cannot protect them against it."

An instant later the monk pushed past Faucon. "May the

Lord save us from all bucolic oafs," he growled irritably as he stopped at the edge of the porch. Then, shaking his finger at the commoners in the yard, Edmund chided, "Impertinent boors! Sir Faucon speaks for our king. He has claimed the boy's corpse as is his right. Defy him, and I promise you that when our justices once again visit your shire, every last soul in this village will be fined for disrespect and disobedience."

Even in the gathering dimness Faucon could see the relief that flickered across Aldo's face. Not only did the reeve understand the tongue of his betters well indeed, he was thrilled with the monk's heavy-handed intervention. Never mind that Faucon was certain his well-educated clerk had no idea what he'd just done.

Bett's challenge had left Aldo no way to submit to an unknown knight claiming unusual rights without demanding proof of those rights. But doing that meant doing exactly as Faucon had accused, calling his new Crowner a liar. To question a man's word was the one insult that always resulted in violence, and violence was the last thing Aldo wanted. Bless Brother Edmund. He represented a higher authority, one that no reasonable man questioned.

Sure enough, the reeve turned to address those standing behind him. "The monk confirms that this knight speaks for our king. We have no choice. We must cede control of Dickie's corpse to them, at least for the now. But I cannot believe that any man— whether this knight or even our king— has the right to bar us from our church. I intend to spend the night here with them. That way, when Dickie rises as we all know he will do, I'll be on hand to help capture him. If any man wishes to join me, he should do so."

"Nay! That's not enough," Bett cried, her tone suggesting she was accustomed to getting her way.

Again she looked at the men standing behind Aldo. "What is wrong with all of you? We are more. Join me! They won't harm us, not when we're in the right and on holy ground. We need only to push past them and do what must be done to

Dickie's body."

"Bett, it's too late for that," one of her neighbors told her as the others took yet another backward step. "We elected Aldo to speak for us, and he has spoken. Now, go home where you belong."

"Aye, protest no more. Go home, else I'll fetch your son to come and get you," threatened another.

Bett glared at them. "If my daughter dies tonight, it will be on your souls," she snarled. Then, spine lance-straight, she turned and made her way toward the churchyard fence, her hems twitching with rage.

Behind Faucon, Will gave a quick laugh. "Now there's a woman I wouldn't mind having in my bed," he muttered.

Chapter Six

As Bett departed Edmund pivoted to face his employer. "Sir, come now," he urged. "We must examine the boy's body while yet a little light remains."

Faucon shook his head in refusal. He wasn't leaving this porch until he'd questioned Aldo, the man in whose smithy the dead boy had been found. The time to do that was now, while the reeve's pride yet stung.

The monk nigh on leapt to his side. "But you must come," Edmund insisted, resting his hand on Faucon's forearm. "Sir, we may be able to tell if the body will walk. There will be telltale marks."

Startled beyond all thought or words, Faucon stared at his clerk's hand on his arm. Not once since they'd met almost two months ago had the monk intentionally touched him. Edmund's hand could have belonged to a saint. His fingers were long and thin, nails carefully pared, and there were no scars to mar his flesh. Then again, Edmund's profession offered its own sort of scarring. Years of scribbling ink onto parchment had permanently darkened the monk's fingers from knuckles to tips.

"What sort of marks?" Will asked in honest curiosity when Faucon said nothing.

Edmund glanced at the elder de Ramis brother. "They aren't described in any detail," he admitted, "but in most of the tales Master Walter collected, someone notices that those who perished after interacting with the living dead were left oddly marked."

"Well, that isn't very helpful," Will offered with a quiet

laugh.

"Sir Faucon," Alf said, speaking over Will, "shall I ask Father Godin to find us torches or lamps? That way Brother Edmund can make his inspection at his leisure."

"Lamps!" Edmund cried, his hand dropping from Faucon's arm as he turned toward the soldier. "But of course! That will do very well. I'll find the priest immediately. When I do, I'll also request he supply us with what we need for the night. We are staying the whole night here, are we not, sir?" he called over his shoulder as he pushed between Will and Alf to reenter the church. There was untoward excitement in his voice.

"We are," Faucon called back, once again feeling the earth shifting beneath his feet. And thus did his confrontation with Aldo end, and his investigation of Dickie's death begin.

"Just as I thought and as we most definitely must." The monk's voice receded as he moved deeper into the church.

Then looking at his brother, Faucon said, "Will, go you with Brother Edmund and see that he gets what he needs from the priest. Perhaps Father Godin can suggest somewhere to house and feed our horses. We'll also need a meal tonight as well as something on the morrow to break our fast. Let him know that I will pay for what we require."

As he said this, Faucon shot a sidelong glance at the reeve. Although it was clear Aldo listened, the reeve didn't raise his voice to offer assistance. That was unusual. Nearly every village headman Faucon had met since becoming Warwickshire Keeper of the Pleas had leapt at the chance to profit in even the smallest of ways from their Crowner's visit.

"I suppose I have no choice if I wish to fill my belly tonight," his brother complained, although there was no bite to his words.

As Will followed Edmund into the church, Faucon offered Alf a grateful tilt of his head to acknowledge the commoner's welcome intervention. The soldier replied with a tiny shrug, accepting his employer's unspoken thanks. "I'll bring the horses into the yard for the moment, sir," he said.

"Milo, go with that man," the reeve said as Alf descended the steps for the grassy yard. "The knight's horses need to be stabled and you have the space. They'll pay for fodder."

At last, something normal on a day turned upside down by the unbelievably abnormal. Faucon released a slow breath along with more tension than he realized he carried. Aldo had just proved himself a reeve like any other, and like all the others, he'd collect his bit of profit from what his Crowner paid to this Rob, and any other villager.

"So I shall, Aldo," replied a thin, balding man in cheerful agreement.

As Milo broke from his neighbors to jog after Alf, Faucon automatically glanced in the direction of where they'd left their horses. Instead, his gaze caught on Waddard limping toward the church. The potter had a crutch under one arm, with his free hand on the shoulder of his eldest girl walking at his side. When Waddard saw Alf and Milo coming toward him, he stopped. His daughter glanced up at him. A moment later, they left the track for the old woman's house, ducking their heads as they passed the cowards clutched at its corner.

Despite the gathering gloom, the grandam hadn't yet closed her door. That said she also watched what went forward in the churchyard, albeit from inside her home. Waddard stepped through the doorway without knocking. As his girl followed, she pulled the door closed behind her.

For the briefest of instants, the urge to rush into the church and speak with Juliana hit Faucon. He released it just as quickly. There was no guarantee the grieving mother would speak with him or was even capable of speaking. However, the reeve was incapable of not talking to his Crowner. Aldo's sense of importance depended on the words that fell from his lips.

"I'm told that the dead boy was found in your smithy," Faucon said to Mancetter's headman.

"He was," the smith replied, both his expression and tone flat.

"Then at first light on the morrow, I'll come to your

workshop. I'd see where he was found and have you describe what you saw when you came upon him. After that, I'll want to speak with any and all in Mancetter who saw Dickie yesterday, especially last night, even if it was but a glimpse," Faucon said.

"To what point?" Aldo asked in surprise.

"As your new Keeper of the Pleas it's my duty to discern who committed a murder— or a burglary or rape— so I know whose estate to appraise for our king," Faucon informed him.

"Well, if that's all you need, you may tell our king that he'll be sorely disappointed by this murder. The one who committed this royal crime has no estate. Dickie's dead father Raymond killed his son," the reeve told his Crowner, crossing his arms before him as he said this. Once again, the reeve was raising a shield to his Crowner.

That had Faucon tilting his head, his brows raised, as he considered the man. "Waddard told me the boy's dead father walks, but that no one witnessed Dickie's death. In light of that, how can you be certain of anything? What convinces you it was the walker, and no other who committed this heinous deed?" he asked, using his words like a mace against the reeve's paltry defense.

Night had closed its fist around them. If it was too dark for Faucon to read the smith's face, he marked Aldo's tense shoulders and the jut of the reeve's chin. The man gave a dismissive huff.

"Who can expect witnesses when the death occurred out of doors in the deepest dark of a cold night? Perhaps on your manor folk are still out and about at that late hour, sir. But here in this vill, every decent soul is where they belong, at home, asleep close to the hearth."

His gaze yet fixed on the reeve, Faucon sheathed his sword. "What of those in Mancetter who aren't decent souls? Where were they last even?"

"What say you?" the big man asked in sharp surprise, pricked by his Crowner's subtle insult.

"I'm simply pointing out that not everyone in Mancetter

was asleep close to their fire," Faucon replied, keeping his tone light. "For certain Dickie wasn't. Rather, he was in your smithy where he died. By your definition that makes the boy an indecent soul. Indeed, the dead boy's mother suggested that the village still believes much the same about her son, before she ran to the church. All of those in the track who called for the boy's body to be desecrated without any proof of evil did so as well. It seems to me everyone in Mancetter considers Dickie an indecent soul. Who else in Mancetter might be his equal?"

The image of that group of youths who had followed Bett's daughter rose with his words. "Tibby perhaps, if what her mother says of her is true? That would be two indecent souls who might well have been outside last night. Were there any other of your folk, decent or indecent, who might have joined them?"

Aldo's arms opened under Faucon's battering. He shook his head in protest. "You misunderstand me, sir. I meant that it makes no difference who might or might not have been outside last night. No one witnessed Dickie's death. But even if there had been a witness, that one would tell you the same thing I have. It was Raymond and no other who did this deed. All of us know that," he insisted.

"What say you?" Faucon directed this question to the five men yet standing behind their reeve. "Was it the dead Raymond who killed his son?"

The old man in the ragged cloak replied first. "I say it could only have been Raymond," he said, confirming his reeve's allegation. "I know for certain that Raymond was on the road last even. I heard him with my own ears."

"But you did not see him with your own eyes?" Faucon shot back.

"Not from inside my house, sir. Nor was I eager to open my shutters as he passed by my window," the oldster told his Crowner, then glanced at the others. "We all heard him, did we not?"

"My wife did," replied the heavy-set man with a shrug.

"For myself, I heard nothing, having already found my bed when Raymond made his journey toward our church."

"I was abed as well," agreed another. "Although this morn my son told me he'd heard Raymond's moans as he passed by our door."

"My daughter says she saw him through our shutters," the fourth and youngest man among them offered earnestly.

That had the oldster shaking his head. "Tom, she's hardly a witness, being but a little lass."

"True enough," this Tom agreed with a rueful shrug. "But she took such a fright after seeing Raymond that she could not be comforted. She cried for much of the rest of the night, ruining our sleep."

"No one at my house saw or heard anything. We all blessedly slept in peace until dawn broke," offered the last man, crossing himself in gratitude.

"What of you, reeve?" Faucon asked Aldo. "Is your smithy near your house?"

The smith nodded hesitantly, still stinging from Faucon's assault. "It is. It stands behind my house in my toft."

"Ah, so you must have heard Raymond and Dickie as they passed by your home on their way to the smithy. What of the boy? Did you hear him cry out or call for help while he fought for his life? Were there any signs around your home that told you how this walker of yours might have forced his living son into the place where he was killed? Could you tell if the corpse used its hand against the lad, or did he take up one of your tools as his weapon? Was there anything to suggest Dickie might have battled for his life?"

These questions spilled from Faucon's lips almost without thought. But then these questions— and the others of their ilk— now framed his every day. The answers they provoked were as spoor in a forest, revealing the tracks and signs that led him to the truth.

Even in the dimness, Faucon could see Aldo gape. "I— I," he started, then cleared his throat. "I didn't see or hear Raymond last night," he admitted grudgingly, then hurried on. "But that's because the boy was bewitched by his father. In that will-less state, he went where commanded without protest. Indeed, when I found Dickie this morn, he sat with his back pressed against my anvil. Sir, I vow it looked as if he'd stumbled and fallen to sit upon the ground. Then while yet trapped on his seat, he'd inched his way backward, seeking to escape something that came slowly at him. Slowly is how Raymond walks," he informed his Crowner.

"Rather than escape his father, Dickie's back met with my anvil. When he could move no farther, that is where he died, in that spot and at his father's hands." Then the reeve added, "God save me, but it chilled me to look upon his face.

"But that's it!" Aldo cried, his arms spreading wide in support of his exclamation. "It's the horror I saw in Dickie's expression that tells me Raymond and no other did this deed! It says that the lad was terrified before he died."

The reeve turned to look at the men behind him. "What say you all? Did you see what I did? A boy who looked as if terror had stolen both the breath from his lungs and the life from his body?" His tone suggested he expected their support.

"I never saw him, Aldo. Father Godin took him into the church and locked the door before I even knew he was dead," the heavy-set man replied. The others nodded their agreement to that.

"Well, terrified is how he looked to me," Aldo repeated irritably when they refused to give him what he wanted for a second time.

"Sir," the reeve said, again addressing his new Crowner, "no living soul is capable of terrifying another into accepting death. More to the point, there's no one here in Mancetter who would have murdered Dickie."

The heavy-set man gave a quiet laugh. "I thought about it," he muttered. That won him a sharp glance from his reeve and a rumble of amusement from his neighbors.

"Didn't we all, Watt?" agreed the oldster, his tone wry.

"But none of us did it," the smith warned, again looking over his shoulder at them before he returned his attention to Faucon.

"Sir, it would be a lie if anyone in Mancetter said they had a groat of patience left for that boy. Me especially, after what he did to my home a few days ago. But none of us would ever have murdered him. Despite what you heard Juliana say, we've done everything possible to help her control her son. We cannot be faulted because our efforts came to naught. How could we counter Raymond, who walked our lane—" the lift of Aldo's hand was meant to indicate the track behind him, "—calling Dickie's name as he came? That sir, is what finally drove the boy to meet the obscene creature that had once been his father. And when he did, it cost him his life." Far too much sincerity radiated from the big man.

Faucon nodded to acknowledge the reeve's words. "I see that you're convinced. But as I said, it's my duty as your new Coronarius and Keeper of the Pleas, to discern the truth behind an unnatural death. Only when I prove to myself who committed the deed will I present that one's name to the jury for confirmation."

"You don't present the name," Aldo corrected instantly. "It has always been my right– the right of the village reeve or headman to present the name to the jury of the hundred when we jurors consider a murder or other crime."

"So it may have been, but no longer. It is now my duty," Faucon replied, offering this as if it had been ordained by the same royal councillors who had created his position out of whole cloth at Michaelmas court last. In all truth, those bishops and barons had given their new Coronarii no instructions at all about the performance of their duties. But Aldo didn't know that, and this was one duty Faucon had claimed for himself and meant to keep.

"Sir, this cannot be," the reeve protested again, sounding shocked to his core. "Not once has our sheriff, or the bishop who was sheriff before him, ever spoken the name to the jury in this hundred, at least not since my twelfth year, when I was bound to our jury. They've always allowed us to do so, thus confirming it as our right.

"For good reason," Aldo continued. "Who knows better than I what any man in Mancetter might be capable of? I know every man's character and what he might do. But more importantly, I know what a man would never do. How can you, a stranger to us in Mancetter, know anything like that about us?"

This wasn't the first time Faucon had met resistance over this point. "I can't and don't expect to know anything about you or your folk," he assured the man. "Nor do I forbid you from speaking a name. Indeed, should you disagree with the name I offer, I insist that you step forward and accuse the one you believe guilty of the deed. However, know that you must do more than shout out a man's name. You must be able to prove to me, as well as to the rest of the jurors, why I'm mistaken about the one I accuse. If you can do that to my satisfaction, you have my word that my mind will be changed and I will instruct the jury to confirm your name."

"But sir, that isn't how it's done," Aldo cried, sounding far more upset over losing what to him was a cherished bit of ritual than relinquishing control of Dickie's corpse.

"Aldo," said the old man, stepping forward to rest his hand on the taller man's shoulder, "we all know Raymond killed his son. If we know it, then if this knight speaks to us, he'll soon know it as well. Let him do his duty. After all, this was a horrible deed and a boy is dead long before his time. Surely, that makes Dickie's death deserving of such scrutiny."

Aldo jerked free of the oldster's touch. "Heyward, darkness has fallen," he said sharply to the oldster. "Be off for home. Aye, we all of us must return to our own families and fires," he told the rest.

Like a troop released from duty by their sergeant, the men turned and departed. The cowards at the corner of the old woman's cottage did the same, turning their backs to their hiding place as they started for the track and their homes. Much to Faucon's surprise, Aldo also turned to depart.

"Reeve, I thought you were staying at the church with us," he called after the man.

Aldo looked over his shoulder at his Crowner. "I'll return with those neighbors who care to join me once I've settled my house for the night. If Father Godin cannot provide you with an adequate meal, send him to me and I'll see to your comfort." There was nothing gracious about his offer.

Chapter Seven

Rather than enter the church, Faucon remained on the porch, knowing that Waddard would be making his way here shortly. Watching the reeve disappear into the darkness, Faucon again breathed out tension. He was surprised to see his breath cloud in the air before him. He hadn't noticed the rising chill, not dressed as he was, in full armor under a heavy cloak.

The instant Aldo was past the far edge of the old woman's cottage, her door opened. A feeble, flickering rectangle of light cut into the darkness, bright enough to halo the potter and his daughter as they exited. The two had barely cleared the threshold before the door closed behind them. Night dropped over their shoulders like a heavy cloak, while the silvery light of a quarter-moon high above them made their faces gleam.

Waddard looked toward the church. When he saw his Crowner, he began limping along the edge of the track toward the churchyard gate. "Sir, have you seen my wife?" he called as he came, sounding beyond exhausted.

"Not since she entered your church. Come, we'll find her together," Faucon invited, then turned to face the nave wall of the church behind him.

The door stood open, just as Will had left it when he'd followed Edmund into the sanctuary. Impenetrable darkness filled the arched opening, unbroken by so much as a glimmer of light. That turned the doorway into more hellmouth than godly entrance.

A frisson of fear crawled up Faucon's spine as his imagination offered him the image of every corpse he'd recently seen, struggling to rise on its own. Then with his next breath, his eyes adjusted and solid darkness resolved into something with more depth and texture. Enough starlight spilled through the doorway to show him the church had a tiled floor, and that there appeared to be three different colors of tiles. The ones that seemed almost black would surely be dark green in daylight, while the grayed squares might be yellow. The final color was definitely white.

From the far end of the sanctuary, a long horizontal white swath moved toward him. His heart quirked, then he cursed himself for a coward and a fool. Squinting made the shape stand still. As it steadied, he recognized the altar table covered with a white cloth. With that, the rest of the small church resolved out of the dimness.

There was nothing along either of the long walls to indicate stations of the cross. However, there were two equidistant lines of wooden posts cutting through the sanctuary. They divided the central open space— the area where the parishioners stood to hear their service— into thirds.

Faucon frowned at the posts. They represented a style of construction used mainly for barns. Then again, given its small size, the church looked more barn than holy structure. That had him agreeing with Waddard. Mancetter's church was too small and too humble for the community it served.

Behind him, the uneven scrape of Waddard's shoes and thud of his crutch across the porch floor marked the man's progress toward his Crowner and the church door. His daughter followed him, moving with a lighter step. As the potter stopped beside Faucon, his girl halted slightly behind her sire.

"The church is yet dark," Waddard said in surprise. "Where is Father Godin?"

"I thought he was in the church," Faucon replied without moving his gaze from the doorway. "He entered ahead of my clerk and no one has exited."

Only then did Faucon recognize it wasn't the thick darkness that unnerved him; it was the complete lack of movement in the sanctuary. Where were Juliana and Father Godin, Brother Edmund and Will? Not even the dead boy moved. Yet.

"Where is everyone?" he muttered to himself.

"Most likely they're all at Father Berold's home," Waddard replied, also staring into the night-cloaked and quiet structure. "For certain that's where Father Godin went after he opened the door for you. Any time he departs Mancetter, he must always hurry home upon his return to assure his wife that all is well and he is safe."

Faucon blinked as he grasped the full meaning of what the commoner said. "The church has a second door?"

Waddard nodded. "Aye, in the sacristy, or rather in the lean-to that serves our church as a sacristy. The door into the lean-to is there, behind the altar." He pointed toward the back left corner of the church.

"Does that second door also have a lock like the one out here?" Faucon asked.

"Nay, only a bar. But a bar is enough for that door if the straps out here are joined." Waddard gave a wave of his hand to indicate the nave door. "As you saw, sir, with that lock in place out here, no one can enter without the key."

That was a sensible enough statement, except for the fact that churches rarely locked all their doors. Nor did Faucon know of any church that sought to prevent folk— alive or dead— from entering by way of the sort of contrivance Mancetter's priest employed. Tucking his gloves into his sword belt, he pulled the heavy door close to him and found the strap fastened above the handle.

It was too dark to see it properly, but his fingers told him it was made of a thin strip of crudely-hammered metal about as wide as his palm. Although the hole that accommodated the lock shank was burred as if only recently cut, rust had formed on both the strap and the metal pins that fastened it to the door. That said the strap had been on the door far longer than Dickie had been dead.

"Was it Father Godin or Father Berold who installed this contraption on your door? Is its purpose to solely keep Raymond from entering the church?" Faucon asked Waddard, again pushing the door wide.

"Neither priest put those there. It was Aldo who created the straps. Nor was keeping Raymond out of the church his purpose for putting them there," the potter replied with another tired sigh. "That's because between his first visit on my wedding night, until this past year, Raymond has returned only every so often, coming perhaps once or twice a year, and content to rattle our latch just enough to disturb me at my rest.

"Despite that, Aldo was convinced that the very idea of a walking corpse on our track was the reason for Father Berold's strange madness, especially because his behavior began the day after one of Raymond's annual visits. Aldo was equally as certain that, if he could make our priest feel safe again, Father Berold would recover. So Aldo hammered out these straps and attached them to the door, borrowing the lock that Father Berold used to close the chest in which he stores his vestments, the holy chalice, and such like.

"Aldo and his contraptions and systems," Waddard scoffed as he shook his head. "He's forever changing the way we do things, always telling us that if we use his method, our chores and tasks will be finished faster or done more easily. He's ever certain his newest idea will be the solution to all our problems, just like that." The potter lifted his free hand and snapped his fingers.

Then he adjusted his crutch under his arm so he could lean more heavily on it as he continued. "That's because Aldo invests far too much faith in his hands and head, and not enough in listening to what the rest of us know. I told him two years ago— and I'd say the same now today if asked— that our priest was already too far gone to ever regain what he'd lost. I, and those who believed the same, have since been proved right. Father Berold only steadily worsens."

Faucon's brows rose as he considered that. "What of

Father Godin? Does he put that lock through the straps every night to protect your church?"

"Him? Nay, not at all. Indeed, he's refused to use that lock until today, only doing so to protect Dickie's body from my neighbors," Waddard replied. "From the moment of Father Godin's arrival here, he's steadfastly insisted that the folk of Mancetter must have access to our sanctuary and our Lord at any hour."

The potter shot a sidelong glance at his Crowner before again aiming his gaze into the darkened church. "Doesn't that just make him as mad as Father Berold? At least about this issue. We've all told him that there's not one of us who'd ever visit the church after nightfall. Who among us wants to open this door and find Raymond waiting inside the church for us? Who wants to meet him along the track as we walk to and from the church?"

"Instead, Father Godin allows Raymond to come and go as he pleases?" Faucon asked, remembering how the Northern priest had suggested that he'd encountered Raymond more than once.

"Hardly so. After we convinced Father Godin that his prayers weren't enough protection for us, he began securing the door every night. Rather than use the lock, he instead threads a length of rope through the holes in the straps then ties it in a simple knot. He's told us that this is as good as that lock. He's seen Raymond's decrepit hands. He says that the corpse could never untangle that knot with his bony fingers.

"We didn't believe him at first," Waddard continued, "but thus far his trick works. Father Godin says Raymond hasn't entered since he began using the rope.

"Well, Raymond hasn't entered the church, but that knot can't stop him from yanking and pulling on the handle. Of late, Raymond has grown bolder. When the door frustrates him, he pounds on it, moaning as he does. A few times he's even walked behind the church to where Father Berold's house stands and pounds on that door as well."

From behind Waddard his daughter made an impatient sound. She started around her father, but in the dark her foot found the toe of her sire's crutch. As his support shifted, Waddard caught her by the shoulder, both to steady himself and stop his daughter.

"Where do you go, Jilly?" he asked her.

Wearing a dark blanket around her like a cloak, she looked up at her father. Moonlight pooled on her round face and made her blue gown glow a pale gray where her wrap didn't cover it. "Papa, the little ones are home with only Evie to tend them." Although her voice was high and girlish, there was a maturity to her tone that belied her age. "Stay here. Sit on the porch and rest. I'll find Mama and bring her to you."

Waddard gasped. "You will not! You'll not enter the church, not by yourself and not until Father Godin brings light to drive away the dark." This was more cry than command.

Between moon and stars there was just enough light for Faucon to see the irritation that flashed across the child's unguarded expression. "Papa, you can't possibly think Raymond could be in there now?! Were we not watching from Grandmama's house while Aldo stood before this very porch? Has this knight not been in front of our church door since the sun set?" Her tone and manner made her sound far bolder than her father.

"But even if Raymond were in there, I'd still enter," the child continued, almost scolding now. "Have you not always told me that Raymond walks more slowly than a merchant's wagon rolls? If that's so, then I can have no reason to fear him, not when all I need do to save myself is to walk faster than he does and not fall."

With that, she pushed her father's hand off her shoulder and strode into the church. "Mama, it's Jilly. Where are you?" she called as she went. If Juliana was within hearing distance, she made no reply.

Faucon followed the child into the structure, making his way up through the central area framed by those roof supports.

Waddard followed, the tired huff of his breath and the achingly slow tap of the man's crutch echoing forward. Ahead of Faucon the girl's skirts rustled softly as she walked, the leather soles of her shoes scraping lightly across the tile.

For the second time, the far-too-still sanctuary set Faucon's nerves to jangling. With no light to guide his feet and the girl's blue skirts just a pale blur in front of him, he moved cautiously. Then from the far left end of the structure came a familiar strained creak– the sound of leather hinges shifting as the door they supported opened.

His gaze tracked the sound, only to catch on the tiny flame that appeared in mid-air behind the altar. Jilly freed a startled gasp and halted abruptly in front of him. Faucon caught himself just before he collided with her. Neither of them moved as that bit of light drifted down toward the holy table.

Just as the scent of burning straw reached Faucon the tiny spark flared into a new circle of light, its purity and clarity speaking of a beeswax candle. Although it was but a small flame, it was illumination enough to reveal Father Godin's face and red hair, as well as the upper portion of the thick candle that played host to it.

Taking the candle, Father Godin turned his back to them. Dark reclaimed the sanctuary for an instant. The priest's footsteps said he moved toward the east wall. When he stopped, he half-turned then tilted the candle away from him. The flame jigged, then stretched toward the ceiling. With a loud sizzle and the stink of burning meat, dirty orange light burst into being. By scent alone Faucon knew the torch had been dipped in tallow.

Bathed in that oily light, Brother Edmund, his face framed by his black cowl, appeared out of the darkness. The monk then bent his torch to the side. A second brand exploded into fatty flame. This time the newborn light glittered against the knitted metal of Will's mail tunic.

"Here be places," the Northern priest said in his odd English. Then, because he spoke in a tongue that neither of his torch bearers understood, the churchman lifted his candle high and waved his free hand in front of it to indicate spots on either side of the wall behind the altar.

While Edmund and Will carried their burning brands where Father Godin indicated, the priest returned to the altar, set the candle upon it, then retreated to that leftward wall. Again, leather hinges creaked. This time, the silhouette of a small door cut into the flickering torchlight. The priest disappeared behind the darkened panel, the hinges creaking one more time as the door closed behind him.

As moths to a flame, the newborn light spurred both Faucon and Jilly back into motion. They continued toward the altar while at the back of the church, monk and knight raised their torches. Metal brackets appeared out of the dark. So did the image of the holy corpus painted onto the east wall. It half-disappeared after the torches settled into their angled brackets and fell a little forward.

At that angle the shifting light spread outward away from the wall. The pool of illumination stretched outward until Faucon saw the full length of the altar dais and the dead boy sitting at its right corner.

Boy? Faucon eyed the corpse propped up against the leg of the holy table in surprise. Dickie was no boy. Mayhap his parents and neighbors had still called him so because of the number of his saint days or some sort of childishness on his part, but it was a man full grown that Faucon saw in the length and breadth of Dickie's corpse.

Just as Aldo had described, Dickie sat with his back straight and his legs outstretched before him. Given his present state of rigidity, his legs extended out into mid-air where they reached beyond the edge of the altar dais. The boy's head had fallen forward as he died. With his chin resting against his chest, his shoulder-length dark hair had spilled over his shoulders to hide his face and the horrified expression that had convinced Aldo that the already-dead Raymond had done the deed.

However, neither Dickie's hair nor the flickering torch light could disguise the matting on the left side of the boy's head or his misshapen skull. Dickie may have been terrified before he died, but fear hadn't killed him. As Father Godin had said, Dickie's skull had been broken.

"Mama!" Jilly gasped from ahead of him, then lifted her skirt to trot toward the altar.

Only then did Faucon notice the spot of blue on the floor at the front edge of the altar dais. Juliana had tucked herself under Dickie's extended legs. She lay on the hard tile floor, her head curled tightly against her folded knees, thighs pressed to her chest, arms wrapped around her legs. She looked as if she'd sought to pull herself into herself, like a turtle into its shell.

"There you are, sir!" Edmund called at the same time. The monk yet stood beneath the bracket that held his torch. His basket of scribbling tools leaned against the wall not far from where he stood. "Have a care as you near the altar. The boy's mother grieves next to her child."

"Brother Edmund, she's finished her grieving for the now," Will said to the monk as he walked toward the altar. He stopped at the left end of the holy table, keeping his distance from a corpse that might rise at any moment while looking at the boy's mother.

As Jilly stopped next to Juliana, Faucon shot a confused glance at his brother, then eased around mother and child on his way to join Edmund. He would have gone farther if he could have, to grant dam and daughter their privacy.

Untoward excitement filled the monk's face as he looked at his employer. "Shall we begin the examination of the boy's body, sir?"

"We shall indeed, but I think we must wait until his mother has left with her kin," Faucon told his clerk.

Edmund freed an impatient breath at that. His arms crossed, he watched as Jilly dropped to her knees beside her mother.

"Rouse, Mama," the girl said gently as she shook Juliana by the shoulder. When there was no response the child again shook her mother. "Mama, come now. You must awaken. The little ones need you." This time Jilly's tone had more of a command to it than a plea. Again there was no reaction from the sleeping woman.

"She's not waking," Edmund muttered irritably. He shot a look at his employer, then glanced at the torch behind and above him. "These won't last all night, sir."

"Give me a moment," Faucon replied quietly to his clerk, then went to crouch beside Jilly.

Even with the altar between him and the nearest torch there was enough light to let him see Juliana's face, or rather the upward half of her face. Tears had left muddy tracks through the reddish dust that coated her cheek. Faucon shook the woman by the shoulder. The eyelid he could see didn't so much as flicker.

"Why doesn't she awaken?" Jilly cried, looking at her Crowner. Then the child dragged in a horrified breath. Her eyes widened in fear as she pressed her hands to her mouth.

Faucon needed no words to guess where her thoughts had gone. He pressed his fingers to Juliana's throat. The woman's pulse was strong and steady.

"I already checked," Will said from his corner of the altar at the same instant. "She only sleeps, although it's a deep sleep for certain."

Startled that Will had cared enough to check on a distressed commoner, and even more startled that his brother might offer commentary on Juliana's state, Faucon stared at his elder sibling.

"Sleep overtook her as swiftly as if she'd taken that potion of mine," Will was saying, his gaze on Juliana. His brother yet stood within reach of the torchlight. That was illumination enough to show Faucon that once again the Will he'd adored was here with him.

"One moment she was weeping next to her son," his brother continued. "The next she'd fallen to the floor and curled into that knot. Fearing the worst, I went to her but her heart yet beat and she breathed easily."

"My thanks for that," Faucon told Will, then looked at Jilly. "There is no need to worry. Your mother only sleeps."

"But if that's so, why won't she rouse?" the child cried in worried protest.

"Perhaps it is her grief," he said to her. "Loss can make folk do strange things, especially when the death is unexpected and fresh."

Jilly shook her head at that. "Her grief is hardly fresh nor was Dickie's death unexpected," she again protested. "Mama has grieved and grieved for Dickie this last year, her tears never ceasing to fall. Now, at last, it's done. The thing she most feared has come to pass. She told me—"

Jilly choked back a sob, then turned her gaze to her sleeping mother. "You promised me, Mama," she said, her voice low. "You promised that if Dickie died, you'd only feel relief, that you'd be happy to know your son was at last safe from all hurt and in our Lord's house. You said that if our Lord chose to take Dickie, you'd at last have more time for the rest of us.

"You promised," Jilly whispered to her sleeping mother, her voice laden with pain. "You must now care for us the same way you have always cared for him."

It wasn't the ache of losing a brother that Faucon heard in the child's voice. Instead, it was the price that Dickie had extracted from his family while he still lived that weighed so heavily on her. That was something Faucon understood well enough. From the moment not-Will had emerged from Will's unnatural sleep, Faucon's damaged brother had extracted his own dear and painful price from his family.

On the heels of that thought came the urge to promise this innocent child that all would be well now that her half-brother was gone. He just as quickly recognized that it wasn't Jilly he wanted to assure. It was himself, or rather the boy he'd once been, the child who continued to hunker deep within him, the lad who persisted in loving his elder brother, despite how Will

84

had sought to hurt him.

"If you wish, you may leave her here with me for the night. I'll watch over both her and your brother. I'm certain she'll awaken come the dawn. When she does, I'll see her safely returned to you. Perhaps for just this night, you and your sister can care for the younger ones and your father?"

The child looked up at him. Her expression had aged with his offer. "So we already do," she whispered, as her slower-moving father finally reached the altar dais.

"She sleeps?" Waddard asked his daughter, sounding both unsurprised and as if he might fall to the floor to join his wife in deep and mindless slumber.

"So deeply that she cannot awaken," Faucon told the man.

"They're trying to decide what to do with their kinswoman, aren't they?" Will again interrupted. "Tell them that if they wish, I'll bear her to their home."

His brother's unexpected show of kindness drove through Faucon like a sword. He cleared the pain from his heart as he cleared his throat. "I'll tell them."

To Waddard he said, "Sir William offers to carry your wife to your house if you wish."

The potter scrubbed his free hand across his brow, then shook his head. "She'd never forgive me if I moved her before she was ready to leave him. That boy was her life," he muttered.

Then Waddard looked at Will. "Thank you for your offer, sir, but nay. She'll stay and grieve beside her child until she's ready to return to us."

Will looked from the potter to his brother, waiting for a translation.

"He thanks you, but says that she should stay here with her son until she awakens," Faucon said.

Jilly dragged in another ragged breath, then came to her feet. She offered Will an awkward bob, then looked at Faucon. "Tell the knight that we thank him, but it's better for us if our mother stays here. If she were unable to awaken at home, it might frighten the little ones."

Faucon nodded, then looked at Will. "The child also thanks you for your offer."

Will started to nod but flinched instead. He brought his hand to his temple, pressing his fingers to the side of his head for a moment. When he let his hand fall back to his side and again looked at Faucon, not-Will had returned.

"Then it seems you've no more need of me here. I think I'll return to the priest's house and see if I can hurry our meal," he said flatly, then pivoted toward the sacristy door. He shot through it so fast that the door bounced in its frame as it fell shut behind him.

Faucon looked back at Jilly. The child had blinked her tears from her eyes. "You vow to keep her safe tonight?" she begged her Crowner softly.

"I so vow," he promised.

"Then it's right that she stays here with Dickie," she replied, her voice still trembling.

Coming to her feet, she went to join her father. "You see, Papa? I told you to let me come here by myself," she said, the tearful child replaced by a sad and sober woman. "Now you've come all this way only to turn and walk all the way home with no rest between. The morrow will see you aching all the worse for it."

Without a glance at her dead half-brother, Jilly started back down the shadowy aisle toward the door, leaving her father to hobble along behind her.

Chapter Eight

aucon came to his feet and watched as father and daughter departed. Jilly's odd behavior nipped at him. Here was yet another unfathomable oddity in a day that had been beyond strange, a girl child who moved through the world with less fear than her father. Then again, having a crippled, fearful sire and a dam obsessed with her only son had likely forced the girl to mature beyond her years.

As for Jilly's bold manner and hard words, that was something Faucon understood all too well. They were the iron from which Jilly had forged her shield, the one she used to protect herself from the many hurts her kin dealt her. Had not he done the same after not-Will appeared out of Will's body and their father had chosen to make him into a knight rather than a monk? However, he'd used the pretense of patience and calm to protect himself from a jealous, half-crazed sibling determined to abuse him. Faucon sent a quick prayer after the girl as Jilly left the church, that their Lord might one day grant her some profit from her pain, just as He had done for Faucon. It had been Faucon's years of pretending patience over Will that had won him the attention of his great-uncle Bishop William, and his new position as Coronarius.

"Sir, the boy's body?" Brother Edmund prodded from behind him.

That brought Faucon around to face the altar and Dickie's corpse. Edmund had moved the candle to the dais floor not far from Dickie's presently frozen hip. Faucon stared at the tall, thick candle in surprise. The series of red lines scored precisely along its length said that this was a timekeeper, a candle for which wick and wax had been carefully weighed so that it would burn for a specific number of hours. Such candles were most common in large convents, where the brothers or sisters needed to know when during the night to sing masses for Matins, Lauds, and Prime. However, such holy houses were also places where there were generally more than a few treasure chests that overflowed with silver. Who in Mancetter could afford to purchase such a candle for their priest, and why, when the folk refused to visit their church at night?

"It won't be easy to see his body around his clothing, not with how he is at the moment," Edmund was saying from where he knelt next to the boy. "I suppose it's a good thing, then, that he isn't wearing much."

The monk's comment yanked Faucon's attention away from the candle and onto the dead boy in front of him. For the first time he looked at the corpse as he would have any other, as a Crowner should. Dickie was dressed only in his chausses, braies, and shirt.

Where was the boy's tunic? Where was his cloak, or whatever he used as an outer garment? God help Dickie, but there were no shoes on his feet! Indecent soul that boy may have been, but he wasn't the poorest of the poor. Only they went out on a cold night during Advent without shoes, and then only because they had no other choice.

Edmund lifted the candle and brushed Dickie's hair aside to better examine the boy's neck. Faucon dropped to one knee next to Juliana, intending to examine the damage done to Dickie's head. But then the monk ran his fingers around the neckline of Dickie's shirt, prying it away from the boy's cold skin. Dried blood flaked from flesh and fabric, spattering onto the altar dais, the floor, and the yet-sleeping Juliana.

"Wait," Faucon said to Edmund. "This is only going to worsen as we continue to examine him. Let me move him away from his mother."

Rising, he took the boy by his bare ankles and pulled the rigid body down the dais. Then shifting Dickie so his damaged temple faced outward, Faucon held the corpse steady and nodded to Edmund. "Now pull his shirt free."

Once the monk finished loosening the blood-crusted linen from the boy's back, Edmund set the candle on the altar above the body. Pulling the neck of the shirt open as far as he could, Faucon's clerk came to his knees and sought to peer down the boy's spine. Edmund shifted this way then that, and even sidled a little. But no matter which way he moved, his shadow followed, standing between him and what he wanted to see.

With an irritated sound, Faucon's clerk sat back on his heels and looked at his employer. "His rigidity makes this so much more difficult. The best I can do is free his shirt from his back. The position of his arms will continue to hold the fabric pinned to his sides. It matters not how I move, I will never be able to see anything well enough to note what might be significant and what is merely a mole or blood. I think we have no choice but to cut away his garments."

The monk's words stirred a strange thought, one Faucon would never have imagined he might entertain until today. "Brother, do those tales of yours explain how a corpse in Dickie's present state can stand and move on its own?"

Edmund's mouth opened. He stared wide-eyed at Faucon for a breath, then pinched his lips shut. Turning his gaze back onto the dead boy, he studied Dickie for a long moment. When he again looked at his employer, dismay twisted his expression.

"What an arrogant fool I am. *Mea culpa*, sir. I have led you astray. This boy won't walk tonight. Look at him! How can he walk? Why did I not realize that before I assured you that such a thing was possible?"

Faucon swallowed his urge to laugh out loud. It was beyond belief that he and a man educated in the world's premier university, a monk who was a master of his art, could be discussing the probability— or improbability— of a corpse walking. That had him wishing he'd known to present this same question to the monk who'd introduced him to the process of *sic et non* while he'd still been at his monastery school. Such a question employed in that otherwise rote back and forth might have captured his interest enough to have made the idea of studying logic appealing.

"Brother Edmund, you know far more than I about this subject, but I have to wonder," Faucon said. "If the Evil One has the power to make any corpse walk, then perhaps he can also animate the yet-stiffened dead by way of the same foul magic that he uses on the long dead."

The dismay softened out of Edmund's expression. His lips shifted into the tight curve that served as his smile. "As always, you see where I forget to look. I learn so much from you," he said quietly.

Faucon blinked in abject surprise. An unbelievable day for certain. "I learn far more from you, Brother. I am always grateful to have you at my side."

The monk's lips quirked upward. "Not so much a penance, I think," he whispered with a nod, then rose to his feet. "Well then, unless you have a knife at hand smaller than your sword, I'd best fetch my basket and find my pen knife."

"Use your pen knife, Brother," Faucon replied with a smile. "I'm not willing to give you my eating knife for this task."

Within moments Faucon and his clerk had moved Dickie to the back wall of the church, directly beneath the image of their Savior in His extremis, where the light from both torches pooled. Fabric whirred as Edmund's keen-edged blade cut through the boy's blood-fouled garments. Once Dickie was bare, Edmund began his examination anew.

As the monk studied the flesh on Dickie's back, Faucon crouched next to the boy's legs and pulled Dickie's hair back from his blood-smeared face. No wonder the lad had caught the eye of a pretty lass like Tibby. Dickie had been handsome, with a broad brow, a long, straight nose, and full lips. His chin was dimpled and his jaw was square, or rather it had been square until one side had been broken.

Faucon then shifted from side to side in his crouch, his

mail tunic rattling lightly against the tiles as he moved. It made no difference from which angle he considered the dead boy's face. There was nothing of terror or horror in Dickie's expression. All Faucon saw was the flattened emptiness common to the newly dead, albeit half-hidden under the smeared gore of a violent attack. That had Faucon wondering if— as often as he now confronted death— he no longer saw the dead the same way others did.

Easing back to sit on his heel, Faucon turned his attention to the left side of the boy's head and the wound that had released Dickie's soul from his body. He pried away the boy's blood-matted hair until he could see Dickie's temple, where the skull had been shattered. Using a finger, Faucon traced the unnatural and broken hollow. There were at least three overlapping, circular ridges. Whatever tool or weapon had been used to kill the boy had either a circular face or base.

He stored that thought with the rest of his pieces, then closed his eyes and again traced the topmost of the circles. As his finger mapped out the shape, his mind's eye offered him the image of a wooden staff, the sort a commoner might use to defend himself. Then again, it might be the head of a small hammer, the sort every smith kept in his smithy.

Eyes still closed, he again explored the shape. This time his finger found something that he didn't immediately recognize. He ran his fingertip over it again. Something soft rolled free of the broken bone and dried blood. Catching it between his finger and thumb, he brought it out to where the light was stronger and peered at the wisp. It was a bit of thread, whether wool or flax he couldn't tell. Uncertain what that meant, Faucon let the bit of thread fall from his fingers as he continued exploring the area of shattered bone. This time, he thought he felt the crisscross pattern of woven cloth.

That had him easing back to look at the boy anew. Of course, Dickie hadn't walked out into a cold night without clothing. Instead, he'd been wearing a cloak with a hood or a cap of some sort when he was attacked. That begged the question of why his murderer might have removed his clothing after his death.

Bringing his finger back to Dickie's damaged skull, this time Faucon considered the depth of the break. The one who had wielded this weapon had done so with strokes meant to crush bone and kill. That suggested a strong man, one as powerful as the smith, who just happened to wish to rid himself and his village of a troublemaker.

As dearly as Faucon wanted to force his pieces to tell him that Aldo had done this, they couldn't. Too much was yet missing. The better question was, could a corpse incapable of opening a simple knot be able to close its bony hand around the shaft of a hammer and wield it with enough power to break a bone?

He drew his finger down the boy's face to his broken jaw. The crack in the bone was almost in line with the temple. With that, he sat back on his heel and considered Dickie's face. While a broken jaw was a horrible injury, one that offered many opportunities death, all of those avenues to the hereafter offered slow and torturous journeys. This attack had been swift and vicious. The point of such an assault was always immediate death.

Nor could the blow to Dickie's jaw have been the first one to fall. Had it been, the boy would have thrashed and fought, making any precision in following blows impossible. That suggested that the blow that broke Dickie's jaw hadn't been intended and had been among the last to fall, which had him reconsidering the precision of those first blows, the ones to the boy's temple. The only thing that made sense was that the first blow had rendered the boy unconscious, if it hadn't killed him outright. Because if it hadn't, that meant Aldo was right and the boy had sat still in terror as he allowed his killer to murder him.

Once again Faucon's pieces shifted and a pattern began to form. He was almost disappointed that when it did, it left Aldo out of its circles. As a former soldier, the reeve wouldn't have bothered with a hammer. Instead, he'd have put a blade in the boy's belly. Nor would he have left the body in his smithy to be discovered. Who did that, when the sensible thing was to move the body to some forlorn and hidden place to rot.

No, this attack had been committed by someone driven by rage. Driven by it, yes, but not completely lost in it. Deep anger had kept the blows focused until the last swing of the weapon, which had gone astray and broken an already dead boy's jaw.

One other thing was certain. If the walking corpse moved as slowly as Jilly suggested, then Raymond would never have managed to land a single blow. How could he have when all Dickie needed to do to save his life was walk faster and not fall?

Releasing Dickie's hair, Faucon looked at the boy's hands. Both had come to rest, palm up. The left one was in Dickie's lap while the right had fallen to the ground next to his right thigh. The right hand, being on the opposite side of his body from the head wound, was almost clean of blood. Faucon picked away what gore there was and confirmed that there were no injuries.

Dickie's left palm had caught a good amount of blood. Faucon cleared away what he could. Although he wouldn't be completely certain until the body was washed before burial, he saw nothing unusual in the boy's left palm.

"Brother, I'm going to move the boy a little," Faucon warned his clerk.

The monk nodded and shifted back to give his employer room to maneuver the corpse. Faucon checked the back of the boy's hands and his arms. There were no fresh wounds.

When Faucon brought the corpse back into position once again, he looked at his clerk. "What say you, Brother Edmund? An unholy corpse is walking slowly toward you, and you're trapped against a wall with nowhere to run. Would you stand with your hands at your sides as the evil creature attacks you?" The question was more rhetorical than a search for an answer.

Brother Edmund frowned. "Who can say for certain, sir, but I'm no warrior. I'd like as not drop to my knees, fold my hands in prayer, and beg our Lord and all His saints for an immediate intervention."

The monk's logical and truthful response made Faucon smile. "I do believe that is what you'd do," he replied. "As for me, because I am a warrior, I'd be more likely to dodge and roll, seeking some way to escape the creature. But here's what neither of us would ever do. We wouldn't sit completely still and let the obscene thing have at us without defending ourselves in some way."

Edmund freed a surprised breath at that. "Why would you think anyone might do that? None of Master Walter's tales suggest this is the common reaction. Even those who are at first frozen with fear upon encountering the reanimated dead recount that they eventually gather their wits enough to battle for their lives."

"That's good to know," Faucon replied. "Yet, I look at Dickie's head and his hands and they tell me that the one thing he didn't do was defend himself. Instead, everything I see says he didn't know that anyone approached him, much less that the one coming toward him intended murder."

"Huh," Edmund said, scowling a little. Then with a lift of his shoulders, he dispensed with this anomaly and returned to his own examination.

Faucon slid off his heel to sit on the floor. With one arm resting atop his raised knee, he stared unseeing at Dickie as he shuffled the pieces he'd gathered thus far. No matter how or where he moved what little he knew, he could see only one possibility. Whoever— or whatever— had attacked Dickie had caught the boy by surprise and rendered him incapable of resisting before going on to do murder to him.

Nothing in that scenario matched Aldo's fanciful tale regarding the boy's last moments. However, it did fit the reeve's confession that he'd heard nothing during the night. Aldo had heard nothing because Dickie had never cried out. He'd never had the chance to do so. But what had the boy been doing in the smithy at that hour?

Behind Faucon the leather hinges on the sacristy door

creaked again. He looked over his shoulder. Father Godin stood trapped in the narrow doorway, held in place by the large tray he carried. It was too wide for the opening. Or rather, it was too wide because of the way the priest held it. The Churchman was trying to turn it on his arm without the use of his other hand, in which he carried a heavy clay pitcher. At last, he gave up and backed out of the doorway, turned the tray and started forward again.

Faucon could see this wasn't going to help. Coming to his feet, he moved to the door as Father Godin again tried entering the opening. This time the belly of the pitcher hit the frame, jolting the tray. The empty wooden cup at one side of the tray toppled, rolling into a round loaf of bread. A bowl slid into a thick slab of ham and a wedge of cheese, then tilted, spilling shelled nuts.

Faucon extended his hand. "Let me take that pitcher, Father," he offered, speaking in his native tongue.

"Many tanks," Father Godin replied in his strangely-accented English and began to extend his arm.

An instant later the priest froze. Raising his head, he met Faucon's gaze. They watched each other for a long moment, then Godin sighed.

"I knew I should have just let them do what they wanted to Dickie," the priest muttered in what was clearly his native tongue, the same French that Faucon spoke.

"I doubt you could have," Faucon replied with a lift of his brows. "If I'm any judge, I think you no more capable of betraying your honor than I."

"Much to my detriment, I fear," Godin agreed. Then still standing in the doorway, the tray braced on his arm, he stared into the darkened body of the church and said no more.

"Who are you?" Faucon asked.

Godin glanced from the monk at the back wall of the church to his Crowner. "I am Godin, presently serving Mancetter as its priest."

"Who were you before you arrived in Mancetter?" Faucon

tried again.

"That is not mine to reveal," the priest who might not be a priest replied carefully, his voice lowered to keep his words between the two of them.

"If not your secret, then your wife's?" Faucon asked.

"Waddard," Godin breathed as he shook his head.

Then his eyes narrowed and his jaw tightened. He raised the pitcher a little, holding it like a weapon. "I am sworn," he warned his Crowner.

His message was clear. Godin would do whatever it took, including spend his life, to shield the woman he protected. Even armed only with a baked clay vessel, it was a far more worthy threat than anything Aldo had presented.

That had Faucon considering what responsibility he, as Coronarius, might have in this situation. He swiftly decided he had none. His duty was to enrich the royal treasury and his king, not confront a well-born man, even one who might be posing as a priest to protect a runaway woman, not unless that man happened to commit a royal crime.

"Why is your English so strange?" he asked.

Godin sucked in a disbelieving breath. Relief dashed across his face. The pitcher wobbled in his grasp, sending golden liquid that looked like cider sloshing over its lip.

Steadying his hand, Godin brought the pitcher back beneath the tray to brace it. "Your man was correct earlier today," he told Faucon. "This is how the language of the commoners is spoken in the far north." His tone was still cautious, as if he yet probed for a hidden trap. "I'm far more fluent in this version of the tongue now than when I first arrived in Mancetter."

"Hard to believe," Faucon said with a quick laugh. "My brother went to find you a few moments ago. Did you see him?"

"I did," the gentleman-priest replied with a nod. "Sir William said his head ached beyond bearing and begged for a pallet or a place where he could sleep. He took some potion, then my—" Godin hesitated "—wife and I aided him in removing his armor. He now sleeps in Father Berold's bed."

Faucon grimaced. Shame on him. He'd been so distracted by thoughts of walking corpses that he hadn't recognized the meaning of Will's hand at his temple. Then he frowned. "How did Will understand you? He speaks no English."

Godin gave a tiny shrug. "What pained him cut so deeply that he didn't notice anything save that his needs were being addressed."

That had Faucon breathing in relief that his brother had chosen to take his potion rather than to run wild. Extending his hand, he said, "Hand me the pitcher. You bring the tray. Perhaps you'll help me disarm as you did my brother, and speak with me as you do. I need to know everything you can tell me about Dickie, about his death, and what you believe happened to him. And I would listen to anything and everything you can tell me about his father, both before and after Raymond's death."

After shedding his cloak, gloves, sword, and belt, Faucon crawled out of his chain mail tunic with Godin's assistance. Then, while he removed his mail leggings and returned his boots to his feet, he watched a priest expertly fold and roll his metal tunic. Taking it from the man, Faucon set his armor atop his cloak, next to his sword, where they would wait for Alf's return with their saddle bags.

Groaning in noisy relief, Faucon stretched. Beneath his padded woolen underarmor, every unscratched itch that had plagued him over the course of his day again cried out for relief. More than anything he wanted to strip down to his braies. But there would be no fire for them tonight, not inside a church. It was wiser, if less comfortable, to avoid getting chilled in the first place.

He looked beyond the altar to the back wall of the church where Brother Edmund continued his inspection of Dickie's body. "Father Godin has brought meat and cheese. Will you pause to join us, Brother Edmund?" he invited.

That brought Godin around in a hurry. The priest looked over the altar at the monk, then glanced toward the sacristy door. Faucon shook his head at the man, moving his hand at the same time to tell Godin that he should stay where he stood.

"I'll happily eat my fill, but only after I've finished my inspection and said my prayers," his clerk replied just as Faucon expected, doing so without looking away from the corpse. Then, yet keeping his back to the altar and speaking to Dickie's chest, Faucon's clerk reported, "Thus far I've seen nothing unusual, or at least not so unusual that it stands out to me."

"Glad tidings, I think," Faucon replied, then sat on the edge of the dais between his pile of clothing and the tray.

Godin remained on his feet, his eyes narrowed. Confusion marked the man's expression. Faucon shrugged. "I knew he would refuse. But not to invite him is an insult I won't do him," he explained quietly.

At that the priest lowered himself to sit on the dais, settling hesitantly at the opposite side of the tray. As Faucon cut a bite of the ham, Godin filled the cup from the pitcher and offered it to Faucon. Cup in hand, Faucon tasted the meat. It was smoky but too salty, more akin to the ham folk used to flavor their morning pottage. Then he took a sip of cider and was disappointed a second time. It was cold and sweeter than he liked.

Sighing, he looked at Godin. "Many thanks for aiding my brother but I must warn you. Although it's likely he'll only sleep, there are times when his pain grows so great it drives him to do strange things. Should you discover him missing or see him run from your home, I pray you come fetch me. And warn Father Berold not to disturb him while he sleeps. Will can strike out if startled awake."

"There's little chance of that," Godin assured his Crowner. "Berold offered your brother the bed and took the chair instead."

Faucon eyed the man in surprise. "So did Raymond drive Mancetter's priest mad as Waddard claims?"

Mancetter's second priest shook his head at that. "It's not madness that afflicts Berold, but some ailment that causes his arms and legs to twitch and fly this way and that. It also affects his speech, making him hard to understand. Although his wits don't seem to be compromised, his memory has steadily worsened during my time here."

"And Raymond brought this affliction on the priest through his visits?"

"Not according to Father Berold," Godin said with another shake of his head. "He said he suffered the same as a child but was healed by our Lord's grace. Then, one day without warning, his limbs again began to move. I pray nightly that he will once again be granted our Lord's touch to either still his limbs or bring him eternal peace."

That had Faucon frowning. "Then why do the townsmen say that Raymond drove him mad?"

Something that might have been amusement flickered through the man's gray eyes at that. "They say it because Father Berold's affliction came on so suddenly and is so strange. It fits well with Raymond's growing legend, and suits their need to frighten each other with the tales they tell. You should know that the truth has little sway here in Mancetter. When I finally understood that— that these folk far prefer their tales over the truth— I stopped insisting that Raymond had never once waited for me right here." He patted the dais on which they sat.

"What?" Faucon asked in a muted pretense of shock. "You did not kneel in prayer before the walking corpse, then watch the obscene thing dissolve before your eyes because of the power of your holy words?"

It was definitely amusement that flared in the man's eyes this time as his Crowner repeated back to him what he had earlier claimed. Godin picked a few of the spilled nut meats off the tray, then rolled them in his closed hand. "I fear not. Indeed, to the best of my knowledge, Raymond has never once been inside these walls."

"And this is because of his hands," Faucon informed the man.

"His hands?" Godin repeated in confusion.

"Waddard told me you have seen the corpse's hands. That's how you knew you needed no more than a bit of rope tied in a simple knot to lock yon door." The lift of Faucon's head indicated the door at the opposite end of the church. "You knew Raymond's bony fingers would be incapable of opening that knot."

"Did I now?" The priest tossed the nuts into his mouth. He chewed, swallowed, and said no more.

Faucon grinned. "I take it, then, that you haven't seen the corpse's hands? A pity. I'd hoped you would confirm that the corpse was incapable of untying a knot. Surely, if Raymond cannot manipulate a rope, he would also lack the ability to swing a weapon with enough force to break a boy's skull."

Godin gave an amused huff at that. "If the first thing is impossible for the dead man, so would the other be."

"I'm told that it was you who bore Dickie's body from the smithy to the church this morning." Faucon kept his gaze on the man's face as he continued. "How was it you knew where to find him and that he was dead?"

Leaning forward to brace his elbows on his knees, Godin focused his gaze on his folded hands between his thighs. He released a slow breath. The silence stretched.

"Brother Edmund would warn you that, as I am the Coronarius for this shire, our king requires you to answer my questions," Faucon told him.

The priest glanced at him but still hesitated.

"The only thing I hunt is the truth regarding Dickie's death," Faucon added, offering the man a quirk of his brows and a small bend of his lips.

Mancetter's acting priest shook his head. "Sir, I'll do my best to answer you, but be aware that just as the king's writ binds you to your duties, so does our Lord and our Church's law bind my tongue. As you've already noted, it's not in me to do wrong even when it serves me.

"I was awakened this morn at dawn by one who warned me that Dickie had escaped his home after the sun had set yesterday and never returned. This one informed me that he was in none of his usual hiding places."

"Which were?"

Drawing a slow breath, the priest said, "A shed on Bett's property and the far barn in Waddard's toft."

Faucon's brows rose. Such places might serve well for a tryst. "Were you also looking for the girl Tibby?"

The priest said nothing. Faucon breathed out in frustration at Godin's careful and too-abbreviated reply, even as his respect for the man beside him grew. "How did you know to go to the forge?" he asked, still seeking the key to unlocking the priest's lips.

Godin sighed slowly. "Here is what you need to know, for I believe it has much to do with what happened to the boy, albeit indirectly. Last month, Waddard begged Aldo to take Dickie on as his apprentice. The boy had failed to master Waddard's wheel, whether due to lack of interest or pure stubbornness, there's no saying. Nor had Dickie ever once given his all to those chores shared by our community."

The priest shrugged. "Everyone here must contribute in some way and for the past year or more, Dickie had been adamantly refusing to do so," he commented, then continued.

"Both Aldo and Juliana were set against the idea for the same reason. Like flint to iron, each time Dickie and Aldo interacted, sparks flew. But Waddard refused to heed them. Instead, he went to his neighbors, seeking their support.

"You see, Aldo's wife was barren. She died two years ago. Although our reeve presently courts Bett, who is recently widowed, she's yet to accept his offer of marriage. That means Dickie is— was Aldo's only heir."

"What?!" Faucon's eyes widened. "Raymond was Aldo's brother?"

"So he was," Godin nodded. "Because of that, every man here agreed with Waddard. I think they had no choice. To deny one heir the chance at what is his by blood is to open the door to denying any other heir that same right."

"Aldo bowed to the wishes of his neighbors. He kept the boy beside him at the forge for all of two weeks before he refused to have Dickie on his property again."

Godin glanced at the man next to him. "Then, three nights ago Aldo caught Dickie in the act of damaging his home. That's why I thought it wise to see if he'd once again visited Aldo with the intent to vandalize. When I arrived, I saw that the gate to Aldo's toft was open, so I awakened Aldo and we went to the smithy."

"How did your reeve seem when he saw you at his door?" Faucon asked swiftly.

Godin's shoulders relaxed with the question, suggesting they'd reached a subject he was free to discuss. "If you're asking if I saw guilt writ upon our smith's soul, the answer is no. Indeed, Aldo was so startled to see me that he didn't think to ask me why I was there. The instant I told him that his toft gate was open he flew out of his door, his feet bare and wearing nothing but his shirt. It was clear he thought the same as I had, that Dickie had done more damage. I followed him as he raced ahead of me into the smithy."

Faucon breathed out his disappointment and set the cup on the floor. "Tell me everything you saw when you entered the smithy. Leave out no detail."

That had Godin frowning in thought. "I don't know that I looked at much other than Dickie. He sat with his back to the anvil, looking much as he does now," the priest replied, the nod of his head meant to indicate the corpse that Brother Edmund inspected. "There was blood on the earth near his feet and on the anvil behind him, but more as if it had flowed from his broken head onto the metal rather than from the attack itself. Beyond that, nothing seemed out of place or amiss. No damage had been done to either the structure or any of Aldo's tools."

"What was Dickie wearing when you found him?" Faucon asked.

That startled the priest. He glanced in the direction of Dickie's corpses, then brought his gaze back to his Crowner. "The shirt and chausses it seems you've cut off of him."

"Were there any other garments, his shoes, a cloak perhaps, nearby?"

"No clothing that I saw," Godin offered with shake of his head.

"Was there anything near him that might have been used to do the murder? A tool, a small hammer, or perhaps a staff?" Faucon asked hopefully.

Again, the priest shook his head. "If there was, I didn't see it. To me, it looked as if Dickie had simply sat down with his back to the anvil and died."

Faucon grimaced at that, for it echoed Aldo's story. "What of the reeve? How did he seem when he found Dickie dead in his smithy?"

Godin met his gaze, then sighed. "You'll think the worst when I tell you," he said to his Crowner. "Aldo stared at the boy for a long moment. Then he shook his head and said 'good riddance.'"

"So, why bring Dickie here instead of taking him to his home?" Faucon wanted to know.

Turning his gaze back to his folded hands, the priest said, "I had reason to suspect that a number of my flock would want to do to Dickie's body exactly what they soon demanded."

Then he looked sidelong at his Crowner. "Here is what I must add to this tale so that you have a better understanding of what happened. Everyone in Mancetter tells me that Dickie is the image of his father. This resemblance was no boon. To some here it made Dickie a constant reminder of his dead father, and Raymond's evil deeds– deeds I'm told that Raymond committed both before and after his death. There are those who despise the boy for no other reason than his parentage.

"Let me add that Dickie has not been a passive recipient of such unfair judgment, at least not since my arrival here. Although I more than once counseled him to choose our Lord's path, one of forgiveness and tolerance, Dickie instead found a number of very clever ways to strike back at his worst critics." The priest who might not be a priest offered a small smile as he said this.

"Who were his worst critics?" Faucon wanted to know.

"Most of the parents of the boys who clung to Dickie and called him friend," Godin replied. "But of all those who spoke against Dickie, Aldo was chief among them. Now don't leap to judge our reeve because of what I've had to tell you. For all that Aldo is rigid and unforgiving, and believes he always knows what's best, in his heart he wants only to do right. He takes his responsibility for these folk as a God-given duty. As quick as he's been to levy fines and punishments for misbehavior, he's just as quick to care for those who have a true need. No one in Mancetter suffers unnecessarily, no one starves.

"That said, no one in Mancetter has been fined more often than Waddard and Juliana, always for Dickie's misbehavior," Godin added.

"So Aldo and Dickie were fighting their own private war," Faucon said softly, offering the priest a small smile.

"They were indeed, a war that was steadily escalating beyond pranks and minor punishments into something more serious," Godin agreed, and again sighed. "I was not the only one here who worried that this war of theirs could end no other way than with a death, and I was certain it wouldn't be Aldo's."

As he continued, Godin again focused his gaze on his folded hands. "There have been wider consequences to Dickie's actions of late. The damage he did to Aldo's home three nights ago may well leave Waddard struggling to feed his daughters this winter, given his present inability to do the work that supports his family."

"Yet, having said all that, you can still insist that Aldo didn't kill the boy?" Faucon asked.

The priest shifted his head to the side to meet Faucon's gaze. "I don't insist on anything. Sir, if this church had a relic, I'd put my hand on it and tell you that I don't know who killed that boy. After that, I'd say to you the same thing your clerk asked at Merevale. Is that not yours to determine?"

Faucon released a frustrated breath. Storing what he gleaned from the man's tale, he cut himself another piece of the ham, then asked, "What of Raymond? What can you tell me of Dickie's father?" And Aldo's brother, he wanted to add.

"I don't know much to tell other than he was Juliana's first husband and Dickie's sire, and known to be cruel and destructive. Everyone who speaks of Raymond is glad that he's dead, preferring his corpse on their lane rather than the man himself."

"Another indecent soul," Faucon remarked, then cut a slice of cheese from the wedge. He offered his knife to Godin so the man could do the same. "Waddard tells me Raymond attempted to break into their cottage, seeking to reclaim Juliana and their son."

Godin returned his Crowner's knife as he nodded. "So Waddard has said to me as well, the tale taking several different forms, depending on the man's mood and how he wishes to tell it. However, the first time he told it to me was the simplest. He said that Raymond returned on their wedding day, or rather the dawn after their wedding night, once all the guests had departed. He said the corpse tried to break down the door to enter."

"Have you seen Raymond walking the track?" Faucon asked.

Again the priest paused before speaking, taking time to choose his words. "I've never seen the Raymond that Waddard described, but that's not to say I haven't seen something on our track. Like everyone else in the village, over the last year I've watched a hooded and cloaked form walk slowly from one end of the village to the other during the dark of night. Whatever lurks beneath that hood and cloak moans as it walks. From time to time, the scurrilous creature dares our Lord's wrath and pounds on the church door."

There was something in the priest's voice that conjured up Jilly and her bold behavior. "These eerie encounters have no effect on you?"

Godin's dark red brows rose. His expression remained guarded. "What effect should they have? The creature, whatever it is, has done nothing more than walk, moan, and rattle a latch. No one has died and no one has been attacked. Not one person has even been sickened."

Faucon took another bite of cheese, chewing on it at the same time he chewed on what Godin had said, and what he hadn't. "Do you tell me that you have no fear in regard to this creature or that you don't fear because you know what actually lurks under that cloak?" he asked after he swallowed.

"Did I say either of those things?" Godin replied in a careful dodge.

Taking up the cup, Faucon sipped cider as he pondered. "Huh," he said at last, "I hope Abbot Henry won't be disappointed. Before we left Merevale the abbot accepted my vow to track down and dismember Mancetter's walking corpse. He promised to help me inter Raymond so he never again rises to torment this village. Now I wonder if once Dickie is interred, Raymond will no longer plague Mancetter."

"I'm certain this village would be relieved if Raymond's visits ended," Godin replied, coming to his feet.

Faucon looked up at the priest who might not be a priest. "Is there anyone in Mancetter you would insist that I speak with regarding Dickie's death?"

"I would insist that you speak with everyone who knew the boy well," Godin replied. "Everyone," he repeated, as if that in some way conveyed a message to his Crowner.

Faucon eyed him. "Tibby?"

"Including Tibby," Godin offered with a nod."Now, I must bid you good night. My wife—" again he stumbled over the word "—doesn't like to be left alone during the dark hours."

"Should I bid you good night or adieu?" Faucon asked.

One corner of Godin's mouth lifted at that. "Were I you, I'd close the church door before it grows much colder. If it remains open, you'll find yourselves hard pressed to stay warm tonight," he said, then turned for the sacristy door.

Chapter Nine

Despite Godin's warning, Faucon left the church door open. He wanted what torchlight escaped it to serve as a beacon for Alf. After eating his fill, he returned to the back of the church and watched as Edmund completed his inspection. At last, the monk set aside the candle and looked up at his employer.

"Although there are bruises, they're old. Other than those, there's nothing remarkable or that I don't recognize on the boy save for these small marks here." There was a hopeful note in his voice as the monk pointed to two faded reddish spots on one side of the boy's neck.

Faucon grinned. "Those aren't the marks you seek, Brother Edmund. Those are love bites, made in the throes of passion, not death." Indeed, those marks proved that if Tibby was ruined, it had been with her permission.

Disappointment washed over his clerk's face. Brother Edmund once again scanned the corpse, then shook his head. "Healing bruises and a few scrapes. Mea culpa once again, sir. I should never have told you this boy might walk," he said on a sigh.

"Why do you say that?" Faucon asked in surprise.

"Because to speak with authority when I lack the knowledge required to *be* an authority is to indulge in the sin of pride," his clerk replied, looking over his shoulder at his employer.

"That's on your soul only if you choose to carry it, Brother," Faucon replied, again fighting the urge to laugh. "I say that your knowledge, even if faulty, of the walking dead has served

108

our Lord well this day. You've prevented these villagers from desecrating a boy without cause, thus saving Dickie from being wrongly cheated of his resurrection. You also prevented these folk from sinning by dismembering an innocent, or at least one who is innocent as far as we yet know. Surely, these two good deeds must counterbalance whatever wrong you inadvertently committed when you offered me your opinions."

"So you might say, but our Lord expects—"

A sharp scrape echoed to them from the far end of the nave. Faucon wrenched around to face the door. Edmund leapt to his feet. Almost as one they stepped closer to the altar, peering across the darkened sanctuary.

The misshapen creature who came toward them had two legs and a great rounded hump on its back. That made its form bulky enough to block the starlight that otherwise filled the doorway. It huffed a little as it moved slowly toward the altar.

"Who comes?" Edmund demanded first in French, his hand pressed against his chest and the crucifix he kept tucked in beneath his habit. "*Qui venit?*" he then challenged in Latin.

"Who comes?" Faucon asked at the same time in English.

"Heyward, sir," called the oldster who had urged Aldo to respect their Crowner's right to investigate Dickie's death. "I come bearing haystraw for our bedding tonight. I know Father Godin hasn't enough to share for our night's vigil and I dare say Aldo won't think to bring any since it doesn't matter to him where he sleeps." There was nothing in the old man's voice to suggest he felt this was a discourtesy on the part of his reeve.

"That's kind of you," Faucon said to him. To Edmund he said, "It's the old man who stood with the smith before the porch. He brings us hay for bedding."

Rather than relief, disappointment again washed over the monk's face. "Huh. I need to pray before I can eat," Faucon's clerk almost grumbled, then rounded the altar.

The old man, his beard as white and thick as the hair upon his head, stepped into the circle of torchlight at the same time that Edmund knelt and disappeared from Faucon's view.

Although Heyward had transported his offering in some kind of blanket, bits of golden straw and sere green strands of summer grass had escaped as he walked, coating his ragged brown cloak and the faded tawny tunic and brown chausses he wore beneath it. With his hands clutched at his left shoulder, holding his bundle closed, his sleeves had slid back to reveal thin arms marked with the dark spots and ropy veins given to the aged.

He stopped a little way from the altar dais. "I fear I didn't have enough sacking to bring to serve all of us." The sideways jerk of the old man's head indicated the fabric in which he'd wrapped his burden. "I'm hoping you and yours won't mind using your cloaks to cover your nests."

"That we can do," Faucon assured him. "Many thanks for doing this." The old man nodded. Then his gaze dropped to the floor in front of him and he sighed sadly. "Ach, Juliana sleeps again. Her and her ever always broken heart, poor thing. Does Waddard know she's here all alone?"

"He does," Faucon replied with a nod. "Waddard deemed it right that she stay, saying she should remain with her son until she's ready to leave the boy. If you don't mind carrying your burden a little farther, would you take it to yon corner?" he asked, pointing to the far corner of the church, away from the sacristy door.

"As you will," the old man agreed.

As Heyward emptied his bundle in the corner, Faucon retrieved his armor and the garments he'd shed earlier, bringing them to the same spot. The old man spread what sacking he had over the pile. When he straightened, his gaze caught on Dickie's body where it leaned against the back wall.

The oldster looked at his Crowner, his brows lifted high over his pale eyes, adding wrinkles to an already wrinkled brow. "Is that how Aldo found him, Dickie without a stitch on him?"

"Nay, we removed his clothing so Brother Edmund could inspect him," Faucon replied. "My clerk is wise with regard to those who walk after death. He says they're often marked in some way. He'd hoped to find those marks so we'd be fore-warned as to whether we needed to bind the boy and set a watch."

"Ah, Aldo mentioned some such about marks as we walked home."

Here, the old man cocked his head. "Well, how you said it wasn't exactly how Aldo said it. He told us your clerk was seeking a mark that only Raymond could have left on his son so there'd be no doubt that Dickie's sire did the deed. Did you find such a mark?"

Everything about the old man— from his voice to the way he lifted himself a little on his toes as he talked— said he longed to inspect the dead Dickie, if for no other reason than to satisfy his own curiosity. It was a gift Faucon could give him, knowing exactly what it would win him in return. "Thus far we've found nothing out of the ordinary. Would you care to look for yourself? Perhaps you'll notice something we missed?"

"If you don't mind," Heyward replied eagerly, already moving to where Dickie's body rested.

With a groan he lowered himself onto one knee. Squinting a little, he scanned the boy. A moment later he reached out as if he meant to move Dickie's hair away from his face. Instead, he caught back his hand and shot an almost guilty glance at his Crowner. Faucon shrugged and nodded.

Heyward pushed aside the boy's hair. Then, just as his Crowner had done earlier, the old man shifted as he sought to study the boy's expression from different angles. "Huh," the oldster said after a moment. "What was Aldo about with that talk of terror? If not for his mouth hanging askew, I'd say Dickie looks like he sleeps."

Then with another groan, he returned to his feet, both knees creaking as he rose. "Sir," he said, "all I see here is Dickie. Nothing unusual, nothing different, save for the lad's lack of clothing." The same disappointment that nagged at Edmund filled the commoner's face. "So what say you? Will the boy walk?"

"What say you, Brother Edmund," Faucon called behind him. "Heyward of Mancetter wishes to know if finding no marks guarantees the boy will stay where he lies."

"I'm no longer willing to speculate," Edmund called back, dismay thick in his voice. "I suppose he'll walk if he walks, or won't if he doesn't. If you don't mind, sir, it's well past Vespers and I must complete my prayers."

"My pardon, Brother," Faucon replied.

To the old man, he said, "My clerk advises that we must do what is usually done in these instances. We sit in the mystery as we wait to see what happens. Now, as I said when you and your neighbors stood before me outside the church, I'd like to speak to you about Dickie's death, and about Raymond. We can do that right now if it suits you." He paused, his brows lifted as he eyed the old man. "Or perhaps you prefer to wait until Aldo arrives before I ask my questions?"

His comment sent scorn dancing across Heyward's well-worn face. The old man's pale eyes narrowed. "You mistake me, sir. Aldo's my reeve, not my liege lord or my master. I don't need any man's permission to speak to whomever I choose about whatever I will. Ask your questions. But know as you do that I'll tell you the same as Aldo did. I'll do that not because it's what Aldo has in any way told me to say, but because it's the truth. Raymond killed his own son."

Heyward leaned a little closer to his Crowner, his eyes alive in anticipation of sharing his tale. "Know that what I tell you tonight is something I wager you'll hear from no one else in this place. That's because I can tell you why Raymond killed his son."

"Why would no one else be willing to speak to me of this?" Faucon asked in wry curiosity.

"Because all of them— every one— are terrified to their bones of speaking of Raymond. They fear that if they utter a single word, they'll attract that godforsaken creature to them. I know better. Didn't I say my piece out loud and before witnesses years ago? Not once since then has Raymond taken any more note of me than he has of anyone else. The worst I've suffered is to have my slumber disturbed by his distant groans and moans."

"Well then, since you're the only one who'll speak of Raymond, speak to me now. Tell me why you believe he killed his son." As he said this, Faucon prepared himself for what he was certain would be a long-winded tale.

Heyward's lips spread into a hard and gap-toothed grin. "Because that bitch's son remains the same mean-spirited ass in death that he was in life. I tell you, sir, if I thought it would help in the least bit, I'd join your clerk at the altar and pray yet one more time that our Lord aids us in ending Raymond's evil visits."

"But there is a way to end them," Faucon told him. "We need only find Raymond's corpse, dismember it, then have it re-interred whilst a churchman speaks the proper words over the new grave."

"And therein lies our problem. We don't know where Raymond's corpse goes to rest after the sun rises. He didn't die in Mancetter," the old man protested.

Faucon smiled at that. "Hear me now. By the time I depart your village, you'll no longer by plagued by Raymond, even if I must run him to ground like a boar."

For one astonished instant Heyward gaped at his Crowner. "By God, sir, you are heaven-sent," he cried. "At last, someone willing to help us!"

"Have you not asked for help before now?" Faucon asked, a little surprised. Being plagued by a walking corpse was nothing to ignore.

"We have indeed. A year ago, when Raymond again walked our track, we sent a message to our bishop. Monks came, but for the whole while they stayed, Raymond made not one appearance. When they left, they said we were confused. They said we shouldn't summon them again until Raymond caused someone to sicken or die. I say Raymond knew they were here and stayed away."

Then the oldster bent his neck to his Crowner. "Sir, a thousand pardons for our niggardly greeting to you and yours this evening. When I tell my neighbors what you've said, everyone, even Bett, will agree that you are well come to Mancetter."

"I took no insult from what occurred earlier this evening," Faucon assured him. "Moreover, I'm pleased to be of use to you and yours. Now, before you tell me what you know of Raymond and Dickie, I say we make ourselves comfortable. Come and sit with me."

Retreating to the hay-filled corner, Faucon shifted the grassy pile to his satisfaction then threw his cloak atop the new stack. He sat, his back braced against the wall behind him, then folded his legs tailor-fashion. As he settled in, the crushed hay beneath him released a faint scent filled with sweet hints of the summer just passed.

"Join me," he invited Heyward, who remained on his feet next to him.

"If you insist and only if you give me your vow to help me rise once we're done speaking. I don't rise and fall the way I once did," the old man laughed as he lowered himself to sit against the wall next to his Crowner.

"You have my vow," Faucon replied, smiling. "So what can you tell me of Dickie's death or his doings yesterday?"

"Naught at all," Heyward said, with a shake of his head as he rearranged the straw beneath him until he was comfortable. He stretched his legs out in front of him, crossing his ankles, then leaned the back of his head against the church wall, his face turned toward his Crowner.

"I never once saw Dickie yesterday. That's because I spent the whole day with my daughter-by-marriage at her parents' house. Well, it's now her house— what with her parents being dead— and my son's along with her. Just as Juliana inherited from her father, so did Nan."

Here, Heyward paused as if mulling over what next to say. "Sir, no offense, but if I'm to tell you what you wish to know

114

and do it rightly, I'll need to tell you more than you're asking to learn," he warned his Crowner.

"Speak as you will," Faucon agreed without hesitation. Then again, why not let the man satisfy himself? He had nothing else to do and he was here for the whole night.

"We've more heiresses in Mancetter than most places. That's because some years ago, our previous lord, in need of more slingers, took a good number of our sons to Ireland with him. He was expanding his holdings there. This he did over our protests and tears. Just as we feared, far fewer of our lads returned to us than departed. But such is war, is it not? I remain grateful that my son was among those who returned.

"Because of that, now at a time in my life when I expected to be a burden to my kin, I yet live in my own home, tending it for a grandson who won't inherit for years yet." Heyward grinned. "Or so I hope. Can't say as I mind too much. I sleep better by myself even in the cold rather than crowded in with six little ones," he offered with a shrug.

"Anyway, Nan, my daughter-by-marriage, and I spent the day shelling nuts and cleaning barrels for her brines, doing it where we always do, at the back of their toft. That's as far from the track as we can be, out of sight and sound of any and all folk who might be moving upon that roadway. I saw no one save my own kin until the evening, when I was once more at my home. That's when I saw, or rather heard, Raymond on the track, just as I told you."

Heyward leaned forward a little, bracing an arm on his thigh, and looked into his Crowner's face. "That's how late it was by the time I made my way home. I'd taken my evening meal with my son's family as I usually do. When I left them, the track was clear, no one else out and about. I'd closed and barred my door and was preparing the embers of my fire to be covered for the night when I caught the sound of Raymond's moans."

"Can you tell me when that was?" Faucon wanted to know.

"After dark as I said," Heyward replied, frowning.

Faucon nodded. "Aye, but do you know whether that was before Vespers or after, or even as late as Compline?"

Confusion filled the old man's face. "I don't know the churchly hours and where they fall well enough to say. Better to ask me if it was twilight or full dark, if the moon has yet to rise or is already high in the sky, or if dawn has begun to drive the stars from the heavens. Last night when I heard Raymond it was after full dark and the moon was already high. Perhaps someone else will know how to name the time by those other hours."

Faucon tried again. "Do you happen to know, then, if Raymond is consistent about when he visits? Or does the timing of his walk change every night?"

That had the old man pursing his lips. Heyward rubbed his bearded chin as he thought. "For certain, over this past year he's been making his walks closer to when dark first falls. But the same time each night? That I cannot say. I do know that the first year he started haunting us, his visits happened closer to dawn. The following year, it seemed he came a little earlier than dawn, but definitely still closer to dawn than midnight.

"And then there were all those years until this one when he didn't visit at all. I've always wondered what happened to prevent him from coming during that span," the old man mused, his gaze shifting to his church's doorway as if he expected the walking corpse to appear in it.

Releasing a quiet breath, Heyward brought his attention back to his Crowner. "But here's the thing, sir. I didn't need to see Dickie yesterday to know what I've always known, the same as I knew a dozen years ago when Raymond first began to walk our track. Raymond always intended to kill that boy. You can ask Waddard. He'll tell you that I said that exact thing to him on the day he wed Juliana. I reminded him of Raymond's curse. I said he shouldn't throw his cloak over Dickie, that he daren't challenge Raymond's ownership of that boy. But Waddard wouldn't listen. He insisted on making the fatherless child he adored his own. This, when Raymond had more than once cruelly abused Waddard during his youth, despising him for a weakling."

"So Waddard has been a cripple since birth?" Faucon asked, seeking to guide the old man toward some of what he sought to learn.

"Nay, not crippled. The pain in his leg began only this year," Heyward said. "Waddard was a weak and sickly child. Had he been born to any other family in Mancetter, we might have asked that they put him out in the wilds whilst he was yet an infant. But Waddard had four older brothers. That's kin enough to bear the burden of caring for a weakling. Then our old lord took three of Waddard's brothers as soldiers, only one to return. While they were away, Waddard's eldest brother, Bill, who had remained in Mancetter, died along with their parents.

"That's when all of us—" the circling movement of Heyward's hand indicated the whole of his village "—met to discuss what to do with a youth who wasn't well enough to care for his father's home or help in the fields, not even a little. Waddard wasn't even fit for tending the geese. Too much time out of doors left him fevered and coughing. Then Juliana's father—"

Heyward paused and looked at his Crowner. "Just so you know, Juliana's sire was also known as Dickie. Juliana chose to name her son Richard after her father, thinking to call him Dickon. None of us would have it, not when we could taunt her sire by calling him Old Dickie. So, of course, her son became Young Dickie," he offered as a grinning aside.

"Old Dickie spoke up then and there, offering to apprentice Waddard, bringing the boy to his wheel. Juliana's younger brother had passed a few years earlier, and Etta, her mother, hadn't once felt the stir of life in her womb after she gave birth to her boy.

"Much to all of our surprise, Waddard proved to have the touch when it came to shaping clay. These days, he does so well that he pays his rents and all his other fees with coins. Everything he and Juliana craft is sold to the tinkers and other merchants who pass this way. Well, and to a few of us as well. That's his pitcher sitting there next to the altar by that tray. Waddard even has coin enough to hire his brother and his nephews to help do the chores that feed his family, the gardening and slaughtering."

Here, the old man gave a sorry shake of his head. "Now isn't it an awful irony that the same wheel that saved Waddard's life and made him successful seems to have crippled him? But who could have known that would happen all those years ago?" he asked of no one in particular.

"Was it Waddard himself, or just his weakness that drew cruelty out of Raymond?" Faucon asked, again bringing the old man back his Crowner's purpose.

Heyward gave vent to a harsh breath. "Waddard's weakness. Weakness was like a goad to a bull for Raymond, driving him to hurt. Some say he might have one day outgrown that, but I don't believe it. Who was going to lead him to change when he had his own troop of supporters, egging him on in his cruelty?"

The old man looked at Dickie's corpse. "That's a talent Raymond shared with his son. Young Dickie also had a way with the lads his age, drawing them to him, making them his own. But unlike Raymond, who created a troop of miscreants and evildoers out of his friends, Dickie's comrades have been nothing but pranksters, the lads doing the sorts of things that most lads will when they're on a lark. Wild for certain, but never vicious. Nor have any of them ever been destructive, at least not until a few nights ago, and only Dickie. For certain, they've none of them ever purposefully hurt another soul.

"Would that I could say the same of my own son. Much to my shame, he was as bad as any of those who became one of Raymond's lackeys," Heyward offered on a sigh.

"Little good shame does me now. At least I can say that the passing of the years has shown me how I and the rest of us in this vill were to blame for Raymond and his evil ways. We stayed silent when we should have raised our voices against him. We stayed our hands when we should have beaten our own sons for honoring Raymond before us. Mostly, we tolerated that boy when we shouldn't have, doing so because of who he was."

"Who he was?" Faucon interjected swiftly, in case the man meant to gloss over this point.

"The son of our then-reeve, Averet. Aye, and it's right that I put most of the blame on Averet, for he must carry that weight despite our forebears' error. You see, my father and our other fathers and grandsires were certain that good would follow good. Averet's father had been an especially good reeve. Thus, they invited Averet to inherit the position without requiring him to prove to us who he was on that day and who he might become as time passed.

"Needless to say, Averet didn't live up to our faith in him. From the first, he took his position for granted, as if it could never be taken from him. Again, that's on us for not raising our voices to remind him that we could elect another in his place. I hope my son's sons will know better than we did," Heyward added.

"So we tolerated Averet in his position, and in how he raised his sons. We said nothing as our reeve turned a blind eye to the misdeeds of his youngest and favorite, while punishing Aldo for doing the same."

That had Faucon frowning in confusion. "But why, if Averet failed you as a reeve, would you now take Aldo in his place?"

Heyward sent his Crowner a quizzical look, then shrugged as he scratched bits of hay off the back of his neck. "Well now, that's because Aldo isn't his father, is he? Despite that Aldo spends too much time thinking about how we do what we do, always forcing us to try ways he swears are new and better, his heart is always with us.

"Truth be told, we were right to elect him. He's not only a better reeve, but a far better smith than his father ever was. As for Averet, if he'd had his way, Raymond would have followed him to the forge and into the position as our reeve. That's why Aldo was glad to leave Mancetter with our previous lord, even though he was no older than Dickie—" A jerk of his head indicated the dead boy at the wall. "—when he departed for war.

"As it happened Aldo stayed away until after Raymond died, although neither he nor we knew that his brother was dead by then. By the time Aldo returned, his father was beginning his journey to whatever reward our heavenly Father intends for him. After Averet was buried, and having no idea where Raymond was, Aldo did as any heir would and claimed his father's home as his own. Not long after that, he also claimed his father's role in our village, with our approval," the old man offered with his thin-lipped smile.

"As for Raymond, even if Aldo had never returned, that boy would never have become our reeve. Nor did Raymond have any future in smithery. Raymond wasn't one who cared to expend his efforts on daily labor."

"Then how did he come to be married to Juliana?" Faucon asked. No father with any sense wedded his daughter to a man who refused to do what was necessary to keep her— and her potential children— fed and housed.

"He had no choice. Raymond took Juliana against her will at a May Day festival, then, arrogant ass that he was, he bragged about what he'd done to his lackeys. He told them all that Juliana had fought him as she sought to protect her virginity.

"When Old Dickie—" Heyward paused, eyeing his Crowner for breath. "In case you forgot, sir, that's Juliana's father. When Old Dickie, learned his daughter was with child by Raymond, he went to Averet and insisted that Raymond claim the babe as his."

"Only claim his son? Weren't Juliana and Raymond married?" Faucon asked, shaking his head in confusion.

"They would have been if Old Dickie had been able to bend his daughter to his will," Heyward retorted with a laugh. "You cannot imagine how hard he and Etta pressed Juliana to stand before the church door with Raymond. She steadfastly refused, even threatening to die by her own hand if they forced her. She said she'd never give Raymond her vow of obedience.

"At last, her father relented and begged her to instead handfast with Raymond. That way, if the babe should die in birth or shortly thereafter, Juliana's betrothal to Raymond could be broken, and she would be free. However, if the babe lived, the child could never be named bastard by any man. Juliana agreed to the handfast, doing so for the sake of her child, even though she trembled at the thought of what the future might hold for her.

"In case you don't know, sir, for us here, a handfast is as good as speaking vows before yon door," Heyward added.

"Well now, you can imagine that as hard as Juliana had resisted their union, Raymond fought even harder to escape it." The old man grinned again, the lift of his mouth radiating a hard pleasure. "The fool! How could he deny the babe after he'd crowed to all and sundry about what he'd done? Nor could Averet ignore his favorite's misdeed, not this time. Much to Raymond's astonishment, his father at last sought to bring his son to heel, demanding that Raymond claim the babe or be banished from his home and our village.

"And so it was that the two wrapped cords around their wrists before witnesses. What Old Dickie hadn't considered was that, after resisting the union, Raymond might immediately press for the right to live with his handfasted wife." Heyward sent his Crowner a knowing look. "I tell you sir, it wasn't Juliana Raymond wanted when he demanded his rights. All he cared about was punishing those who had forced him to go where he didn't wish to be.

"His request took Old Dickie aback for a bit. There was no one in his household who wanted that boy inside their walls. But what could they do? Raymond was Juliana's bound husband. There were witnesses. Worse still, Old Dickie now worried that Raymond, as husband to his daughter and the father of his grandchild, might actually inherit what belonged to him one day."

The old man's blue eyes sparked with wicked amusement as his brows lifted. "I vow to you that the fear of having Raymond as his heir is what sparked Old Dickie's inspiration. He told Raymond that he could have everything he wanted after a year and a day, but only if Raymond met Old Dickie's conditions. He demanded that Raymond spend every day of the next year working at the wheel save Sundays, holy days, our ale days, and those days when he was required to work in the fields. Old Dickie warned that if Raymond missed so much as an hour of labor, he'd be evicted from their home, and Juliana would be disinherited.

"As you might well guess, sir, Raymond wasn't having that. Thwarted, he ran from Mancetter. For the fortnight or so that he was gone, Averet was crazy with fear and grief. When Raymond returned, he was wearing another man's cloak, and carrying a haunch of some forest meat."

Shaking his forefinger, Heyward leaned closer to Faucon. "Others will tell you that this is how Raymond chose to support his son, by bringing meat to his wife's household. I know better. Becoming a thief and a poacher was how Raymond meant to punish his father for forcing him to handfast with Juliana. Averet, who was ailing by then, fretted terribly that the boy he loved best would lose his life for his crimes, which was rightly what happened."

Having offered his opinion, the oldster continued with his tale. "Then, just as the end of that year approached, Raymond left Mancetter not to return for almost a full year. That gave Old Dickie the right to terminate his daughter's betrothal to Raymond. He came to all of us who had witnessed the handfast and we agreed with him, that Raymond had abandoned his wife and child. It was at that same time that Old Dickie invited Waddard into his home as his apprentice."

Heyward looked toward the altar, at the corner where Juliana slept. "I'm not certain which Waddard wanted more, the security and income that Old Dickie's wheel represented for him, or the possibility that he might one day call Juliana his wife. I think he'd had his eye on her from an early age. Not that Juliana wanted him. Our Lord knows well enough that after what Raymond had done to her, Juliana didn't want any man. Well, any man save that boy of hers.

"Despite how he—" again, a jerk of Heyward's head indicated Dickie's corpse "—was made, she loved her son more than anything in this world.

"When Raymond once again deigned to visit us almost a year later, he was livid to discover Waddard residing in what he thought of as his home. He demanded that Old Dickie wed Juliana to him. No matter that Raymond didn't want his wife or son, he didn't want any other man near them either. That was Raymond, the sort who'd break a tool rather than let anyone else use it," he said on a harsh breath.

"But Old Dickie didn't flinch, not even when Raymond threatened violence. He told Raymond that all of us in Mancetter had agreed that he'd forfeited his rights to Juliana and Young Dickie. Old Dickie then told Raymond that if he wished to complain, he'd have to do it to the sheriff or the monks at the manor house. Those were two things that Raymond dared not do by then, not given the trade he'd chosen to ply. Thwarted, that vicious ass vowed there and then to kill Juliana and his son if she dared to wed with another man."

Again the old man fell silent. This time, as he lost himself in the past, his gaze drifted toward the darkened arch of the doorway across the church. He sighed. "And didn't Raymond reappear the day after Juliana finally traded vows with Waddard? He did his best to tear down the walls of their cottage, trying to reach and destroy what he still thought of as his."

"Alive or dead?" Faucon asked swiftly.

The old man shot him a startled look. "Why, dead of course. One of the merchants who comes through here regularly, one who has known and dealt with both Old Dickie and Waddard, brought the news six months before Waddard and Juliana were wed. He said he'd seen Raymond hanged for his crimes with his own eyes. I think he said it happened at Killingworth, the sheriff's castle."

Heyward shook his head. "As I told you, the dead Raymond was no different from the living man."

"Did anyone witness the corpse tearing at their walls?" Faucon wanted to know.

"There were those among us who heard the commotion, but most of us had only just then found our beds. By the time anyone realized something serious was afoot, the sun had arisen and the corpse was gone. Still, we could all see the damage Raymond had done to their home," Waddard said.

"Thus," the old man continued, "Raymond having found his way home after death, has returned once again to do what the man had done in life, seek to frighten and belittle us. He makes his way through Mancetter again and again because it pleases him to persecute those he thinks of as beneath him.

"This is why I know that Raymond killed Dickie," Heyward told him, his tale circling around to its end, "doing so for no other reason than to hurt Juliana. As Aldo told you, Raymond had been bewitching Dickie, seeking to lure his son close enough to steal Dickie's life. That he has at last succeeded should surprise no one, especially because his attack happened at this time of the year."

Faucon frowned at the old man. "What has this time of year to do with Dickie's death?"

Heyward sent his Crowner a disbelieving look. "From whence do you hail?"

"Essex, in the east," Faucon replied, "although I'll someday inherit land here in Arden through my lady mother."

"Well then, since you'll one day be a neighbor, let me be the first to warn you. This is the time of year when Herla and his army marches on Watling Street. When those immortals ride in their Wild Hunt, all the dead become uneasy in their graves, while those like Raymond, who have the ability to move, become even more powerful," he informed his Norman better.

A thrill of fear shot through Faucon only to be followed by a rush of curiosity. "I think I would like to see that army on the Street," he murmured.

Shock dashed across Heyward's face. "You would not! Although I was just a boy the one and only time I saw that ghostly army, I'll never forget so much as a horrible instant of it. One of the marchers looked at me as he rode past. His eyes were as black and empty as the night. I tell you, my blood ran cold!"

That did nothing to quench Faucon's growing desire to bear witness to the riding dead. He brought the old man back to his task. "Did you ever hear Dickie talk about his father calling for him?"

Heyward blinked as he thought. "Well, I'd be lying if I said that boy and I had the occasion to speak much. But my son said that Nan, that's my son's wife, had heard from Bett's cousin that Tibby had told Bett that when Dickie heard his father's voice he became like one who walks while lost in sleep, with no will of his own. Tibby said that while Dickie was in that state, he had no choice but to do whatever Raymond bade him. According to Nan, Tibby also swore to her mother that Dickie was under Raymond's evil influence when he tore great holes in Aldo's home just a few days ago.

"That made sense to me," the old man added, his eyes alight again with the pleasure of one who loves to tell a tale. "Such a deed would have pleased and amused Raymond, satisfying his need for cruelty. He drove his own son to ruin what his older brother loved, while also causing Waddard to have to empty his purse to repair the damage."

Again, Heyward glanced in the direction of the sleeping Juliana. "Aldo told me that Juliana was beyond rage when she learned what Dickie had done to our smith's house. Aldo said if he hadn't seen her for himself, he wouldn't have believed she could get that angry. He says Juliana asked him to send for the sheriff. She wanted to let Sir Alain take Dickie to his gaol so he could rot and die there, just as his father had."

The old man gave a lift of his shoulders. "Or so Aldo told me. But knowing Juliana, like as not she'd have thought the better of her threat before long, so great was her love for that boy. Instead, Waddard intervened. He begged his wife to relent. He said it wasn't fair to punish Dickie when it was Raymond's fault, having bewitched him. And we who are his neighbors had to agree with him."

Faucon turned this piece of Heyward's tale over in his mind. For certain, this explained Juliana's reaction to Waddard this evening. The husband she had never really wanted had stepped between her and a boy she thought of as hers alone.

Just then the distant rumble of male voices echoed into the nave. Faucon shifted to look at the church door. Torchlight flickered and bobbed in what he could see of the churchyard framed in that opening, the light coming steadily in the direction of the doorway.

"It seems your reeve and neighbors arrive for our vigil," Faucon told Heyward.

Chapter Ten

"Do they now?" Heyward replied, an eager note in his voice. "Help me up then, sir, if you don't mind."

Faucon came to his feet, then offered the oldster his hand. By the time Heyward stood upright, the first man had entered the church. It was Watt, the heavy-set villager who had joined Heyward and Mancetter's reeve in confronting their Crowner prior to sunset. Dark of hair, his graying beard reaching the center of his chest, he wore a green tunic and red chausses. Like Heyward, he brought straw caught in a thick blanket over his shoulder, with a large, stoppered jug caught in the crook of his other arm. The clay vessel was the same color and style as the pitcher Godin had used to serve his cider. Watt's wide grin and easy nod of greeting to Heyward and an unknown knight belied any fears he might be harboring over what might happen in the coming hours.

Entering on Watt's heels was Tom, the slightest and youngest of the men who had earlier stood with Aldo. Wearing a tunic and chausses in mismatched shades of blue beneath his brown cloak, Tom's round face was framed by his thinning fair hair and a patchy beard. Like Watt, his expression was alive with anticipation rather than dread. He bore a basket in one arm and a woven hempen sack in his other hand. Whatever that sack contained was large and round, and heavy, for it strained at the weave.

Faucon didn't recognize the two men who followed. Both were tall and thin, with dark hair and beards. Their long faces and narrow features were similar enough to proclaim kinship.

One carried a jug in one hand and more blanketed straw over the other shoulder. The other held a torch in each hand. Both torches smoldered and shed dirt, saying the man had sought to smother them just before entering.

"Bertie! Is that your plum wine in that jug?" Heyward called out with a laugh.

That had the man carrying the jug grinning. "You know it is, Heyward. When Gervis here—" the movement of Bertie's head indicated his torch-bearing kinsman— "said Watt would be bringing his swill, I decided I'd come with something decent to drink or the night would drag."

Edmund stood up on the other side of the altar. Exasperation filled his face. "I think I'll go to the priest's house. Perhaps he has a prie-dieu I can use," he told his employer

"Of course," Faucon said. "Return when you will, or I'll send for you if you're needed."

As Edmund departed through the sacristy door, Mancetter's reeve entered the church behind Bertie and Gervis. The big man had thrown a cloak over his shoulders to ward off the cold during their vigil. Rather than baskets or jugs, he carried a goodly length of rope and folded hempen sacking.

As Aldo saw the old man standing next to Faucon, he stopped short. "Heyward, what are you doing here?" There was a hard edge to his voice.

"Waiting for all of you to arrive," the old man called back, as if startled by the question.

That had the smith striding swiftly up the nave. He made his way around the four men who had entered ahead of him— they'd stopped to gawk at Dickie's corpse leaning against the back wall— without a glance in the direction of his dead nephew. Nor did he look at the sleeping Juliana even as he stepped carefully around her.

"I thought we agreed you'd stay away from the church tonight," Aldo said to Heyward, as he halted in front of Faucon and the old man.

Eyes narrowed, the oldster crossed his arms. "Well Aldo,

I recall that you mentioned something of that nature. But I doubt I agreed. Had I, then I expect I wouldn't be here, would I?" he told his reeve sarcastically.

That had Faucon's brows rising. Despite the faith Heyward claimed he and his neighbors put in their reeve, Aldo clearly ruled the unruly.

Heyward's comment stirred the other men back into motion. After depositing their burdens in the back corner they came to stand with their reeve. "Why would you want to keep Heyward away, Aldo?" Tom asked for the rest.

Aldo's gaze flickered to Faucon. Faucon's brows rose in understanding. The reeve had proclaimed himself the one man in this village who knew exactly what its folk would and would not do. He'd commanded Heyward away because he knew all too well that the garrulous old man would come to the church ready to spill all he knew. But Faucon had heard nothing unexpected in the old man's story. That had him wondering what Aldo feared Heyward might say.

"Because we'll be here until dawn, Watt," Aldo said to the heavy-set man, "and Heyward will likely want to depart come midnight. Which of you wants to walk him home, knowing that you must then walk back here alone in the dark of night?"

"Why would I leave before dawn?" Heyward protested indignantly. "Am I not a man like the rest of you, and just as capable of taking part in this vigil? As for needing an escort to my house, I'm not a doddering idiot. I daresay that from here I could find my way to my door on a moonless night during a gale, neither of which plagues us tonight."

"And who will protect you if Raymond attacks?" Aldo shot back.

Although the old man's chin lifted and his arms remained tightly crossed in front of him, his brow folded in confusion. "Why should any of us fear Raymond now? You said it yourself, Aldo. Your brother finally has what he's always wanted, his son's soul and Juliana's broken heart." Heyward aimed the jerk of his head in the direction of Dickie's mother.

"What reason has Raymond to return to Mancetter now, much less bother me?"

"I was wrong to say that," Aldo retorted. "Now that I've had time to think about it, I see that Raymond instead intends to redouble his efforts to destroy us. That's why he killed Dickie. He'll call his son to his side. With both of them sharing a hatred for us and our home, they may well succeed!"

Heyward gaped at his reeve in astonishment. His neighbors all shifted so they could better see their smith. Surprise and confusion marked every man's face.

Outrage drained from the old man. His arms opened. "Aldo, this isn't like you. What's wrong?"

"There's nothing wrong. I'm simply trying to protect all of us from further harm." Although the reeve's voice was firm, there was a strained edge to his words.

"But that's why we're here tonight, isn't it?" the man Bertie asked, rearranging his grip on his jug of wine as he spoke. "It's on us to see that Dickie doesn't escape these walls, not just to protect us from him, but to see that he doesn't flee to where his father might wait for him. Because we're here, they'll never be able to join forces."

"Isn't that the very purpose for bringing your rope and those sacks of yours?" added Gervis, the plainer of the two tall men, the one still holding the smoldering torches. "We're to bind and blind the boy so he can't escape."

"Well said," Heyward replied to the two men with a nod. "And Aldo, know that if by some evil miracle Dickie does elude all our attempts to hold him here, this knight—" he pointed to Faucon "—stands ready to do exactly what we intended earlier. He'll dismember the boy in our church, then on the morrow fetch Merevale's abbot to come to weigh the lad down in his grave with the proper prayers."

"So I have vowed," Faucon offered, stepping into the fray for no other reason than to further provoke the embattled reeve.

His English words won startled looks from Bertie and

Gervis. He nodded to them. "I am Sir Faucon de Ramis, our king's new servant and Keeper of the Pleas in this shire. Although I came to Mancetter to determine who killed Dickie and call the jury to confirm the name of his murderer, I vowed to Abbot Henry of Merevale that I would also hunt down Raymond, dismember him, then return him to a grave where he will remain eternally confined."

"So you see," Heyward said as Faucon fell silent, "if Raymond has any sense left in that rotted skull of his, he'll never again set foot within our bounds."

Grateful astonishment filled the faces of all Heyward's neighbors save Aldo. "God bless you, sir, for offering to do this for us," Tom cried.

The reeve loosed a scornful breath. "Tom, what makes you think this knight will have any more luck than we in finding Raymond's lair?" he chided harshly.

"How hard can he be to find?" Faucon asked, glancing at the men around him. "I'm told the corpse moves more slowly than a merchant's wagon. At that speed he should be easy to track, even in the dark."

"But sir, he uses magic to escape anyone who tries to follow him," said Watt. "What was it, Aldo, about two months ago that you, Bertie, and Gervis trailed that cursed creature as he left Mancetter?"

"So we did," Bertie said, leaping in to play his role in a cherished tale. "He remained right in front of us as we walked the track, then turned to enter our western field. Of a sudden he began to move much faster, then just like that—" he lifted his hands the way Godin had earlier done to demonstrate how Raymond had disappeared, "—the earth swallowed him up."

Gervis nodded. "Aye, and didn't we walk in circles for a goodly while looking for him? Yet we found not a trace. It happened so quickly. One instant he was right in front of us. The next, he was gone."

"Did you find any trail or sign of his passage when you returned the next day to where you'd last seen him?" Faucon asked the man.

Both Bertie and Gervis stared blankly at their Crowner for an instant. That made them look all the more alike. "We didn't return to the field the next day," Bertie said after a moment, then looked at his reeve. "Aldo, why didn't we think to go back the next day to search?"

"What could we have found?" Aldo snapped, his brows lowered and his mouth curved downward. "Raymond disappeared in the middle of a field that had been walked by every man and beast in Mancetter."

"Aldo, why are you acting this way?" Watt asked.

"What way?" Aldo snarled like a cornered wolf.

"Like the ass end of an ox," Heyward retorted. "By the bye, not only are you behaving like an ass, but there's something wrong with your eyes. You said that you saw terror on Dickie's face when you found his dead body in your smithy. Well, I looked at him. There's nothing in his expression that speaks of terror."

For the first time since entering the church, Aldo's gaze flickered in the direction of the boy's corpse. The smith flinched. "That's just what I thought I saw," he said, blustering again.

"I want to look for myself," Tom said. Setting down his sack and basket, he went to where Dickie sat. Watt followed.

"What does it matter?" Aldo called after them. "If I'm wrong, it's only because I was barely awake when Father Godin and I found him." This time there was no mistaking the panic in the man's voice.

That had Faucon rising to the balls of his feet, grateful that he'd chosen to leave his boots on after disarming. Tom crouched before Dickie. With Watt leaning forward to look over his shoulder, and both Gervis and Bertie peering at the boy from where they stood, Tom pushed aside the boy's hair, exposing Dickie's bloodied face.

"Ha!" Heyward crowed in satisfaction. "Just as I said. No terror in his expression."

Aldo took a backward step. Faucon leaned a little forward. Even as he readied himself to give chase if required, he was certain the reeve wouldn't run. Aldo would have to be a fool to think he could escape. If nothing else, the smith wasn't a fool.

"What does it matter?" Mancetter's smith almost pleaded, shaking his head like a man stunned. As he took another backward step, his gaze again flickered toward his Crowner. "Have it your way, Heyward. I was wrong. It wasn't terror that I saw," he said, his hands lifting to show he yielded.

"Aldo, we all know what a terrible liar you are," Gervis told the man, speaking gently as he watched his reeve in surprise. "Why do you try to lie to us now?"

"I— I," Aldo stammered and took another backward step.

Even in the meaty, oily light of the torches, Faucon could see the color drain from the reeve's face. The big man took one more backward step. His heel hit the dais edge. Crying out, he dropped to sit on the altar platform. The rope slid from his shoulder. The sacking beneath his arm dropped to the tile floor.

Aldo raised his head to look up at his neighbors. "I no longer have the right to pronounce the name of the murderer to the jury," he cried, his voice breaking. He pointed at Faucon. "Instead, it's now the duty of that knight."

"What has that to do with anything?" Watt asked in frowning confusion.

"Aye, why should that eat at you? We all know it will be Raymond's name he speaks," Heyward agreed.

"Whose name do you think I will pronounce, Aldo? Yours, perchance?" Faucon asked at the same time.

Aldo looked up at him. "What does it matter how I answer you, sir? Even if I could convince you that my dead brother killed his son, you'll never speak Raymond's name. How can you? You are the king's servant! A dead man without a coin to his name isn't going to satisfy you or your royal master. Our king demands his fines. He requires a life to pay for a life."

As Aldo's charge assailed both Faucon's honor and his pride, he stiffened. "Do you dare claim that I intend to falsely accuse you?" he demanded.

"God help me, but that's not what I mean," Aldo cried, sounding truly bereft. "This must be the work of my brother. Raymond has finally found the perfect way to punish me for taking what he believed belonged to him. He killed his son in my smithy three days after I caught Dickie in the act of housebreaking. The men from the far end of our hundred don't know me. If they hear that much and you don't speak my name, they'll believe I paid you not to say it. How can they think anything else? They don't know how Raymond torments us! I'm ruined no matter who says what." As he fell silent, Aldo buried his face in his hands.

Faucon's insulted pride deflated with the smith's words. This was the legacy of Sir Alain's corruption. But discarding Aldo as a suspect in Dickie's murder left Faucon feeling almost as disappointed as Edmund over the lack of special marks on the boy's corpse. Sighing over that, he settled back into the business of the Crowner.

"Answer me now and speak the truth," he commanded the reeve. "Did you kill the boy?"

"Of course he didn't," Heyward said, speaking for Aldo. "I see now that I hadn't thought it through completely, sir. Aldo is right. It wasn't just Waddard and Juliana that Raymond meant to destroy, but his brother as well. He must have known you were coming," the oldster assured his Crowner.

"Answer the knight, Aldo. Did you kill the lad?" Gervis asked over the old man as Tom and Watt returned to stand with him and Bertie. Gervis's gaze shifted to Faucon as he continued. "Not that we could blame you if you'd murdered that boy, Aldo, considering all the rancor and disrespect he's shown you these past months."

Aldo lifted his head from his hands. His expression was bleak. "Here in this church and before God, I swear that I did not kill Dickie," he vowed, his gaze moving from man to man as he spoke.

Bertie nodded. "That's enough for me. I'm convinced Aldo

did no murder. What say the rest of you?" He looked at his neighbors.

The other men nodded their agreement. "Aldo's word has always been good enough for us," Watt said, speaking for all. "We in Mancetter will all stand with you, Aldo, and proclaim your innocence to the jury, and after that to the king's justiciars."

Heyward looked at Faucon. "Raymond and no one else did this," he insisted yet one more time.

Setting his jug and blankets on the dais, Bertie picked up the rope and sacking that Aldo had dropped. "Now that we've settled the matter of Aldo's innocence, I say we bind and blind the boy. Then we can get onto the rest of our night and someone can open a jug. It'll be mine first, Watt," he told the man.

"Mine is better than yours, Bertie, and you know it," Watt retorted with a laugh.

"You'll have to let us be the judges of that," Heyward said, grinning as he joined the other four men moving toward Dickie's rigid corpse.

Chapter Eleven

Faucon waited, expecting Aldo to rise and join them. Instead, the reeve remained seated on the dais edge. He looked as deflated as Faucon felt. Faucon went to sit with the man.

Aldo kept his gaze on the floor in front of him as he said, "You don't believe that Raymond killed his son. I can see it in your face."

"I cannot say what I believe as of yet," Faucon replied. "But consider this, Reeve. What if I discover that your dead brother didn't do this deed? Will you be like Heyward and continue to insist, even though it means the one who truly killed the boy lives undiscovered among those you seek to protect?"

Aldo straightened at that. He frowned at his Crowner. "Sir, if it were anyone other than Raymond, I'd know," he again insisted. "This much is true— although no one had any patience left for Dickie, no one here wanted him dead. Not even me."

Then he added, "Well, truth be told, as Watt said earlier, I thought about his death, especially after he broke my wall."

"What of Bett?" Faucon asked. "Dickie ruined her daughter. Could she have crept from her home last night and killed the boy?"

"Nay," Aldo replied far too quickly.

That had Faucon cocking his head as he eyed the man. "How can you be so certain?"

The reeve watched him for a moment. "It's no one's business but ours," he said, his voice lowered. "I'm certain Bett

136

didn't kill Dickie because she spent the night with me last night, staying until just before dawn. It's a miracle that Father Godin hadn't seen her on his way to come tap on my door."

Faucon blinked in surprise, then was surprised by his surprise. Where else save from her reeve would the woman have found permission to behave so boldly? "So you have more than a few indecent souls here in Mancetter, after all," he told the reeve. "What say you? Were you willing to walk back alone in the dark after escorting her home?" he offered in a gentle taunt.

The corners of Aldo's mouth lifted. "I knew the moment those words were out that I was a fool to say them to you. It was almost dawn and she chose to walk home without me." He sighed. "Fool I am, and a doomed one at that. Not only will both my brother and his son likely haunt me for the rest of my days, but after what happened at yon door tonight, I think I've lost Bett as well. I doubt she'll ever forgive me for sending her away from the church."

Faucon swallowed his laugh. "As if you had any choice in the matter. She was beating you bloody with her words."

"She did that for certain," Aldo agreed with another sigh. "So much of what has happened is my fault."

This time, when the smith looked at the knight next to him, Faucon at last saw the man in whom these villagers had entrusted with their lives and fortunes. Any man with courage enough to shoulder the responsibility for his errors was a man with enough courage to risk his life for another if called to do it.

"I knew two years ago that Dickie would never find his proper place here with us," Aldo told him. "There are too many who can never forget my brother and what he did. They despise Dickie for no other reason than his blood. Although I knew the right path to take, I couldn't bring myself to force it on the boy or on Juliana, not after what—" The reeve fell silent and again turned his gaze to the floor.

"Where did you intend for that path to take Dickie?"

Faucon prodded.

"Well away from his mother and Mancetter," Aldo replied. "Dickie needed to leave, both for his sake and ours."

Faucon's brows rose at that. He glanced at the sleeping woman. She had held her son close for too long. Now, if Edmund was proved right and Dickie did walk because he'd interacted with his dead father, then he'd remain eternally beyond her reach. "Where would you have sent him?"

Aldo gave a quick lift of his shoulders. "I know men who yet serve our old lord. I was a slinger for him until I took this," he touched the scar that cut down the side of his face. "After that, he found me more useful to him in a smithy. I remained in his employ until I received word that my father ailed, and returned home.

"Dickie is– was excellent with a sling, never missing what he aimed at. But when I mentioned to Juliana that Dickie would make a good soldier, she refused to hear me. I told her it was unfair to keep him trapped here where he was a constant reminder of the dead man who tormented us.

"But I waited too long before making my suggestion," the reeve continued. "Had I offered this option to Dickie the previous year, he might have spoken up for himself and defied his mother. But by the time I found the courage to broach the subject with Juliana, Dickie wanted only one thing— to defy me. He refused my offer for the sole reason that I made the suggestion.

"That left me no choice but to try one more time to find him a place among us, since he had failed at Waddard's wheel. When I assigned him to drive birds from our newly-sown fields, he lay on his back and stared at the sky. When I set him to watching our sheep, he let them break into our barley field, claiming he'd fallen asleep. I put a hoe in his hand. In the time it took Watt's boy to finish two rows, Dickie had barely finished one, and done as poor a job as possible. No matter where I put him, he made himself useless to us, to me."

Aldo freed a frustrated breath. "That would have been

tolerable had Dickie been a lackwit. He wasn't. Instead, it pleased him that I knew he was using failure to taunt me. He remained undeterred in his defiance no matter what sort of punishment his misbehavior earned, including me taking the rod to his back. Each punishment only made him more determined to resist me. Raymond had been the same when he was Dickie's age. Perhaps this, rather than affection, was why my father ceased trying to control him," Aldo finished quietly, then fell silent.

Leaving the reeve to his own thoughts, Faucon watched the other village men wind their rope around Dickie's rigid body. As they worked, they discussed the virtues of knots and which one might best serve this purpose.

"Did Heyward tell you that Waddard forced me to take Dickie to my forge?" Aldo asked a moment later.

"I did hear that," Faucon replied, unwilling to name Godin as the one who brought him that tale.

"Here again, I failed that boy," the reeve confessed. "Waddard was right when he went to our neighbors and recruited them to confront me. And the others—" The lift of his hand indicated the men at the back of the church. "—were right to stand with Waddard and demand that I comply with his request."

Aldo shook his head, then looked at Faucon. Pain filled his blue eyes. "My God, you cannot know what a hell it was, having that boy beside me, day in and day out. He was his father's son in so many ways, even his voice. After a few weeks, and although I could see that he might well have a talent for the work, I could bear his presence no longer. My prejudice ended Dickie's apprenticeship.

"And just as Raymond always did when thwarted in his desires, Dickie went mad in rage. He threw my tools, over-turned buckets and benches. He screamed at me, saying I had no right to deny him his inheritance. When he refused to calm, I carried him out of the smithy. Let me say that was no easy feat. He left me as bruised as I left him. That night Dickie returned and tore great holes into my front wall."

"Shame on me," Aldo said softly. "I pretended outrage over what Dickie had done, when I knew it was as much my fault as his."

"Not Raymond's?" Faucon asked. When the reeve sent him a confused look, he clarified. "Dickie's father didn't bewitch his son into destroying your home?"

"Oh, that," the reeve said, sounding embarrassed. "Another thing I shouldn't have said, not even in my panic. That tale was the one time I knew for certain that Dickie lied. It was Tibby who gave it away. She stood with him as he spewed his falsehood, then swore she'd heard Raymond's voice as he called for Dickie. Then she went too far and said she'd watched Dickie fall under Raymond's spell. She told the others that he'd walked like a dreamer toward my home.

"I knew better," Aldo told the knight next to him. "I'd caught Dickie with his fist through my wall. He was in no way befuddled when I put my hand on the back of his neck. So I asked Tibby how she'd come to witness Dickie's enchantment when it happened well after the time she should have been abed."

Again, the corner of the reeve's mouth lifted. "That's when it was Bett's turn to go mad. She— we hadn't realized that on the nights Bett visited me, her daughter fled their home, leaving her younger brother alone, to meet Dickie in the dark."

"Well, that explains how the girl managed to meet Dickie without being missed," Faucon said. "How did Dickie manage the same thing when he comes from a household that includes two adults and five little lasses?"

"That I cannot say, sir," Aldo replied. "But as you note, he managed it more than once. I know for a fact that had Juliana ever noticed him missing, she would have raced up and down the track, crying for all of us to come help her find her darling boy."

Faucon freed a disappointed breath at that. "Tell me this, then. Father Godin said he saw blood on your anvil, but didn't notice anything else about or around the boy's body when the two of you discovered him. Did you find the weapon or tool that was used to end Dickie's life?"

"Raymond used—" Aldo stopped himself. "The one who did this used my smallest hammer. All my smaller tools hang on the short wall that frames the opening to the smithy," he added in explanation. "I found it on the floor not far from the anvil. It made sense that Raymond might have taken it from the wall as he entered. But I was certain he'd left it out in the open to taunt me."

"What of garments or shoes?" Faucon asked.

"No clothing," the smith said, then came upright with a start as he sent a startled glance at his nephew's corpse. "But all he wore was his shirt and chausses," he said in surprise.

"Aye, not even shoes on his feet. That's hardly seems likely, considering the boy walked from his house to yours on a cold night," Faucon said. "Perhaps you can tell me this. From what I can see, your nephew either sat or stood still as someone, whether alive or dead, hit him in the temple more than once until he was dead or mortally wounded. From what you've said of him, I cannot believe he would have allowed this without trying to protect himself in some way."

"True enough!" the reeve retorted. "If Dickie felt at all challenged, he struck first, whether with words or his fists. That's how certain he was that everyone in this village meant to attack him. I can testify that he was more than able to defend himself using either."

"Then how is it that he's dead now?" Faucon murmured, frowning in thought.

Aldo shot him a surprised look. "You know as well as I, sir. He's dead because it was his time."

The reeve's pragmatic statement caught Faucon by surprise, not because what Aldo said wasn't true. It was. Their heavenly Father knew every man's time. It was he who had changed. Somehow, he'd begun to think of the murdered as having been cheated of their lives.

Yet considering this, Faucon shifted to look at Dickie's corpse. At the wall, either Bertie or Gervis, Faucon couldn't tell which one, was pulling the sacking over the dead boy's head and shoulders so his corpse would be unable to see to escape.

And just like that, two more of Faucon's pieces— the bit of fiber he'd found at the boy's temple and the crisscross pattern imprinted on his skin— found their places. Father Godin had said the moaning figure that walked the track did so hooded and cloaked.

Dickie hadn't seen his attacker because he'd been wearing a hood that limited his field of vision.

"What are you doing to my son!" Juliana shrieked from directly behind them. "Take that sack off him!"

Chapter Twelve

Aldo wrenched around so swiftly his shoulder hit Faucon, knocking him to the side. As Faucon scrambled to his feet, the five men at the back wall turned. Juliana was on all fours at the corner of the altar. Her knees caught in the folds of her skirt, she scrabbled and slid as she tried to rise.

Standing, Aldo leaned down to put a hand on her shoulder. "Stop, Juliana," he told her gently. "We're doing what you know we must."

She shoved free of her reeve's hand and fell back to seated. "Take it off!" she screeched. "Take it off him!"

"Not until dawn and we're certain," Aldo told her, again reaching for her. "Let me help you up. I'll take you home."

She slapped his hand away. Her face was hollow and her gaze oddly unfocused, enough so that Faucon wondered if she was fully awake. Again, Aldo reached for her.

She flailed at him. "Not you! Don't you dare touch me," she snarled. This time she found her footing as she sought to rise. Staggering and stumbling, she started toward the back wall.

Aldo glanced at Faucon, then trailed the woman, making no attempt to stop her. Faucon followed.

"Get away from Dickie," Juliana shouted at the men standing between her and her son.

Instead, they joined their arms and made themselves into a wall, Watt at the center. "Juliana, you know we cannot," he said to her, his tone not unkind.

With a piercing cry, she threw herself at the man. "Take that sack off him!" she wailed, shoving against his chest.

"Sweetling, you shouldn't be here. Go home to your girls," Heyward told her from where he stood next to Watt.

The grieving woman launched herself at the oldster. He cried out as she hit him and fell into Tom. Bertie grabbed for Juliana. She ducked and thrust into the opening where Heyward had stood. Tom and the oldster again locked their arms, trapping her between them. She strained steadily forward. Just as she wrapped her fingers around the corner of the sacking on Dickie's head, Aldo caught her at the waist and pulled her back from her son.

Crying out, she writhed and kicked. Her neighbors all danced out of harm's way. Aldo lifted her then grunted as her heel caught him in the thigh. Faucon shifted closer, ready to catch her should she win free. Just then she fixed her hands on Aldo's restraining arm and folded at the waist.

"Watch yourself!" he warned the reeve.

Too late. She sank her teeth into Aldo's arm. Yelping, the smith's hold on her loosened and she slid free.

The instant her feet touched the tile she was moving. Aldo reached for her at the same instant as Faucon. They stumbled into each other. Juliana ducked under their arms and raced for the door, howling as if in agony.

"I've got her!" Faucon shouted to the others as he chased after her.

At the church door, his fingers brushed her arm. With an ear-piercing shriek, she plunged out into the dark and leapt off the porch. Arm yet outstretched, Faucon followed, only to slide as he hit the grassy turf.

"Juliana, stop!" he called after her, using her given name when he had no right, hoping to startle her.

By the time they reached the far end of the churchyard, he was again within reach. She exploded through the opening then threw the gate back at him. It bounced off, but the damage was done. Scrambling to regain his stride, he watched helplessly as Juliana, a pale blur in the dark in front of him, gained yards in the track.

She flew past her mother's home only to stop stock still. Her form melded with another patch of darkness, then she screamed in terror. The thought of a walking, murdering corpse drove Faucon to greater speed.

Etta of Mancetter threw open her door. "Juliana! Where are you?" she shouted in panic, hurrying into the track.

"Sir Faucon?" Alf called at the same time, then huffed as Juliana gave another wordless shriek.

"Hold her, Alf," Faucon commanded, giving thanks to all that was holy.

Cottage doors along the track flew open. Firelight spilled from some, including the one across the pathway from Etta's home. Framed in that light were Tibby and Bett.

Etta started up the track toward the sound of her daughter's voice. "Who's there?! Juliana! Where are you?!" she begged, her voice trembling with fear.

"Mama, they put a sack over his head to make him look like Raymond," Juliana keened.

Panting, Faucon trotted along the track toward Alf. As he passed the old woman, he said, "Your daughter runs mad with grief. I'll take her home."

"Nay, bring her to me!" Etta called after him.

Much as Aldo had done, Alf held Juliana in front of him, but he'd managed to fold her arms behind her back. She now sagged against his hold, her head bowed. Although her shoulders shook as if she sobbed, she made no sound. Then her knees buckled. Alf let her sink to kneeling in the roadway. She hung as a child's poppet from his hold.

"I've got the saddlebags, sir," Alf said quietly.

"Then I'll take her," Faucon replied and gathered the woman into his arms.

Rather than fight, Juliana sagged into his embrace. Her breathing was quick and shallow. It seemed she'd once again catapulted into that strange sleep of hers. He looked up the track at Waddard's home, yet thinking to bear her back to her family. But, unlike their neighbors, the potter's cottage was dark and still, its door closed. It was Jilly's hesitance over her mother's odd sleep that had him turning in the track toward

Etta.

"Up here," Juliana's mother commanded Faucon as she retreated to the doorway of her home.

With Alf following, Faucon carried Juliana up out of the track. The old woman stepped aside as they reached her door, allowing them to enter ahead of her. Faucon moved a few steps into what he expected would be the usual living space given to these sorts of homes. Instead, he found himself in a dark narrow space with walls close by on all sides. Without a flicker of light to show him where he should go, he stayed where he stood. Alf shuffled to an abrupt stop behind him.

Outside the house Etta shouted, "Oh, close your doors and leave us alone. Especially you, Bett." Her call was followed by the sound of distant slams. Then, stepping inside, Juliana's mother closed her door, plunging the narrow space into total darkness.

Her footsteps scuffed. The bar thudded into its brackets. Faucon looked behind him and saw nothing but the blank darkness of Alf's night-cloaked form.

"Why have you stopped?" the old woman asked from the door, her voice heavy with tears.

"You'll have to show me the way," Faucon replied.

"Then move aside so I can pass."

Both Faucon and Alf turned sideways. As his back met the wall behind him, Faucon felt the outline of a shutter rather than a flat surface. Etta slid past them and disappeared around a corner. When Faucon followed, trusting she knew where she was going, he found the big room he'd expected to see from the doorway.

Although cloaked in heavy shadows, he made out a table at the right wall, while the left wall was cluttered with various shapes that could only be the barrels and bags containing Etta's stored foodstuffs. At the far end of the room he saw something solid and rectangular, no doubt a bed.

Ahead of him, Etta stopped. Faint tendrils of warm air reached out to him from the center of the room, suggesting the usual placement of the hearth. Baked clay clattered as the old woman removed the *covrefeu* from the embers it had shielded. Their red glow was light enough to show Faucon that her hearth was raised to about knee height.

Leaning down, the old woman blew on the hot coals. Tiny flames awoke, revealing the smooth coat of plaster that covered the pedestal. Again, Etta blew on the ashes. This time he saw the open framework surrounding the hearthstone itself. There was an iron grate set across it at just the right height for simmering.

The old woman tossed a handful of something onto the coals. With a whoosh and a crackle, the flames doubled in size and number. Brilliant sparks scattered upward, borne aloft on writhing wisps of smoke reaching for the hole in the ceiling. As they flew, they made their way between her rafters, casting their brilliant, brief light on the smoked meats, long braids of onions and garlic, and great bunches of dried herbs that hung there.

As the fire strengthened, Faucon looked at the woman in his arms. Juliana yet hung limp in his embrace, her head turned a little toward his chest. Her eyes were closed and she made no sound. When he didn't hear her breathe, he jostled her a little. Although her eyelids never moved, her chest lifted ever so slightly and she freed the whisper of a sigh. He shook his head. Indeed, she once again slept like the dead.

"Goodwife, where shall I put your daughter?" Faucon asked.

That brought the old woman up from the hearth and the task of awakening her fire. Faucon recognized Juliana's narrow face in Etta's but there was a softness to the old woman's features that her daughter lacked. Faucon wondered if this was a result of age or because Etta had lived a sweeter life than that of her child.

Moisture glistened on the old woman's wrinkled cheeks. Using the back of her hands, Etta scrubbed away her grief, replacing tears with dark smears. Her loosened hair shifted around her as she moved. The newborn light found a few remaining glints of gold in her white tresses. So too, did it outline her form through her short, thin garment.

Alf walked past Faucon to the hearth and set down the leather saddlebags he carried. "If you'd like, goodwife, I'll feed your fire for you while you fetch a gown," he said in what was both an offer and a warning.

Etta gasped. Whirling, she hurried toward the far end of the room. "Sir, come this way. You can put my daughter in my bed. It's there against the wall. If you don't mind, would you remove her shoes?" She now sounded as worn and heartbroken as Waddard.

While Etta took her gown from a peg in her wall, Faucon went to the old woman's bed. Such as it was. Etta had left her blanket tossed to one side when she'd run to her door. The mattress beneath it was nothing but a well-worn sack, no doubt stuffed with hay, atop a wooden frame about as high as his knees.

Settling Juliana onto the mattress, he pulled off the woman's shoes, then settled the blanket over her. This time she didn't even sigh. When he turned, Etta stood between him and the hearth. She now wore a dark green gown. Her fingers flew as she plaited her hair. Her gaze was on her daughter.

"She sleeps like the dead," Faucon told her.

"She does that from time to time, ever since—" Juliana's mother paused, then frowned in confusion. "But I don't understand. You and she came from the church. Waddard told me he was going to take her home."

"So he intended," Faucon replied. "But Waddard found her sleeping in much the same way as she does now, so deeply that your granddaughter couldn't awaken her. Because of that, he decided it would be best to leave her near Dickie until she awakened naturally and prepared herself to leave her son."

Etta's fingers stilled in their task. Her eyes narrowed. Her jaw tightened. "That coward," Waddard's mother-by-marriage breathed harshly. "Never once has he behaved toward her the way a husband ought."

Then she caught her breath, as if realizing she'd spilled a private thought. "Forgive my careless tongue, sir," she apologized. "I'm not myself today. Nor have I any right to complain. Whatever his faults, my son-by-marriage is a good man. He loves my daughter and my grandchildren. He's even provided me with my own home," she said, tying off her plait. She sounded more bitter about than grateful for Waddard's generosity.

Faucon smiled, seeking to put her at ease. "Such is family, always the good to balance the bad, eh?"

Rather than smile in return, her eyes filled. As her grief again overflowed, she bowed her head to hide her tears, then turned to walk back to her table. Faucon followed.

Alf yet stood at the hearth. When he caught his employer's gaze, he gave a jerk of his head toward the table as he touched his belly. His brows rose in question. They were coming to know each other very well. Faucon nodded.

"Goodwife," Alf said, "by chance would you have any bread and meat that Sir Faucon could buy for our supper?"

Standing at her table, her head yet bowed, Etta again scrubbed her pain from her cheeks. Then, sucking in a shaken breath, her shoulders squared as she pulled together the broken bits of herself.

She looked at her countryman. "I beg your pardon, goodman. What sort of hostess am I, especially after the boon you just did my daughter? Of course I'll find you and your knight something to eat."

"Are you certain? Perhaps we should leave you to your rest," Faucon demurred, giving the response required by the rules of courtesy, when leaving wasn't at all what he wanted to do.

Etta shook her head at that. "It's not that late. And now that I've reawakened my fire, it will burn for a time. To tell the truth, sir, I doubt I'll get so much as a wink of sleep tonight," she continued, her voice quavering in grief. "This, when I well know I'll need my wits about me to watch the little ones on the morrow."

Reaching down, she pulled out one end of a bench that was tucked under the table. "Sit, sir," she invited Faucon. "I'll not only find you something to fill your belly, but you'll stay here to eat it. And I'll not take so much as a groat from you for it. But I fear that today was such a day that I've nothing hot to offer you," she told them. "Will you have yesterday's bread toasted with lard, and a cup of fresh ale?"

It was a truly generous offer, for hog fat was a precious substance. "That sounds like a feast to me, goodwife," Faucon replied, sending Etta another reassuring smile. This time, she managed a weak twist of her lips in return.

As she turned to the wall behind the table, where shelves and pegs held her kitchenware, Faucon arranged the bench so Alf could join him at the table. Etta returned with her knife, half a round loaf of bread, and a clay jar covered with a cloth. But when she lifted the knife to slice the bread, it quivered in her hand the same way her mouth trembled. The set of her shoulders said that she again struggled to control her grief.

"Larded bread toasted over the fire was my mother's favorite," Alf told the old woman, returning to his feet. "I learned young how to make it, and never once disappointed her when I did. I'd be happy to make it for us. Shall I cut you a slice as well?"

With a nod, she offered Alf the knife. "There's a skewer at the hearth I use for toasting," she told him, her voice muted.

"My mother used a skewer as well," Alf replied, as if startled to discover this wasn't an uncommon practice.

As Alf sliced the bread, Etta returned to the wall and found two wooden cups. These she carried to the corner of the room opposite her bed. Turning on the bench, Faucon watched as she filled the cups from a large jug.

"Goodwife, Heyward mentioned your daughter's troubles with Raymond," he said, thinking to ease his way into the questions he needed to ask.

Instead, the old woman came upright with a start. She

pivoted to look at him. Liquid dribbled down the side of one cup.

"Troubles?" she snarled. "If by that you mean Raymond took my daughter against her will and put Dickie into her belly, then aye, she had trouble with that spawn of the Devil. He destroyed her life, stealing all the joy from her soul. Then, as if that wasn't enough, he returned in death to again torment her.

"Why did Raymond choose her?" she asked harshly of no one in particular. "She never favored him. She never once so much as showed her ankles when he was near, not like that lightskirt Bett."

"Yet, I'm told that your daughter found joy in Dickie despite how he was made," Faucon said gently.

"A joy she's now lost forever, again because of Raymond," Etta retorted.

Then she turned her back on him to finish filling her cups. Her shoulders began to shake. "What if Dickie's passing is the death of my sweet girl?" This was a muted cry.

"Won't love for her little lasses support her in her grief?" Again Faucon spoke as gently as he could.

"I can only pray it will be so," Etta replied, returning to the table.

Once she set the cups before Faucon and Alf, she wiped her eyes with her sleeve, then brought the skewer to the table. Alf handed her a thick slice of bread spread with the lard. She began to thread it onto the iron rod, but her hand trembled so badly the bread broke. With a sound that mingled both rage and pain, she sent the skewer and crumbs sliding across the table.

"Why her? Why my child?" she again demanded.

As Alf took up the skewer, Faucon offered the woman his cup. Etta stared at it for an instant, then pulled a stool out from beneath the table. Sitting, she wrapped her hands around the small wooden vessel and drew it close to her chest, then stared unblinking at her tabletop.

"You were listening when I spoke to your neighbors at the

church door," Faucon said to her. "You know that it's my duty to discover who murdered Dickie. Do you know anything that can help me do my task?"

"What help can you possibly need? Raymond killed him and that's a fact," Etta said flatly without raising her head.

"So I'm told," Faucon agreed. "But there are things I don't understand and as of yet no one has explained them for me. For instance, how did Dickie come to be in the smithy after dark last night?"

That had her frowning at him. "Raymond had been bewitching my grandson. He must have called Dickie to him so he could kill him."

"Aye, but surely as one bewitched, Dickie shouldn't have been able to escape his home without awakening his parents. How could they have not heard his steps or their bar being moved so he could open the door?"

"Who can say how that evil magic works," the old woman replied, looking confused by his question.

"I'm also told that Bett speaks the truth, that Dickie had made Tibby his. So too, have I learned that the two did their trysting at night. Here again, Dickie fled his home without being discovered. How is that possible?"

Outrage replaced Etta's confusion. "As if Bett has the right to demand redress from my daughter's family over what her child has done!" she snarled, her blue eyes glinting in the low light. "What did she think would happen when she left Tibby and little Sim alone at night while she went to futter Aldo? That whore."

Faucon cocked a brow at that. So much for Aldo's secret. Had the reeve really believed he could hide his liaison in a place like this?

"Aldo would marry Bett in an instant, although only our Lord knows why he wants that bold bitch," the old woman added. "But she prefers not to remarry while still wishing to take her pleasure in Aldo's bed. Hear me! If Tibby is maiden no longer, as Bett claims, then I know it was by her own choice.

That girl's a roundheels, just like her mother."

As Alf took the skewered bread to the fire, Faucon watched Etta sip her ale. When she set the cup back on the table, she sent a sad glance his way. "But that's not what you asked me. Would that I could tell you how that boy managed to slip away unnoticed. I'm certain Juliana couldn't have known he was gone, for had she, she would have moved heaven and earth to stop him. As for Waddard, I'm not sure he would have questioned Dickie even if he'd seen that boy pass him for the door.

"That man! It's Waddard's fault that Juli's been beside herself these last months. Rather than help her while she sought to save her son from himself and his bad blood— a hopeless task, for sure— Waddard instead prevented anyone from punishing that boy as he deserved. It was Waddard more than Dickie who was nigh on driving Juli into madness."

The old woman shook her head. "It befuddles me how my daughter can still love that child after all the harm Dickie's done. Whenever I'd tell Juli that she had to let him go, that he was nothing but his father's seed and sure to wend his way to hell one day, she'd protest that Dickie could and would change his ways.

"That she might hold so tight to him after all that is an even bigger mystery to me," Etta continued harshly. "What I— and everyone else here— knew on the day that child was born, we all still know. Dickie was fated to come to the same evil end as his sire."

Taking another sip of ale, she looked at Faucon. "Do you know that three nights ago Dickie broke Aldo's house?"

"I do," he said, nodding.

She offered a nod in return. "As awful as housebreaking is, I was beyond grateful that the boy had finally done something so destructive. At last, I said to myself, Juli will see him for what he is. Now she'll be willing to apply the rod with vigor, not only because he deserved it, but to drive at least some of Raymond's influence from Dickie's soul.

"Then I prayed that my daughter would at last banish her son from our vill. For a brief moment I thought our Lord had heard me," Etta told Faucon. "I vow I'd never seen my daughter as angry as she was when she looked upon Aldo's ruined wall. She told our reeve to send for the sheriff. But then, when Waddard had no right to it, he interfered one more time. Once again he pleaded for mercy on Dickie's behalf, and once again Juli let her husband bend her to his will," she finished on a disgusted breath.

Etta was silent for a moment. "Would that my husband had never brought Waddard into our house. Waddard is the reason Raymond returned to haunt us. Even though my Dickie had broken Juli's betrothal to Raymond, and even though Raymond had left our village, we all knew that Juli dared never marry another man. Hadn't we all heard Raymond vow to kill her if she ever lay with another man, even if he had to come back from the dead to do it?

"But when we received word that Raymond was dead, Waddard insisted the threat was over. I knew better. So did Juliana. But Waddard begged and pleaded, vowing that he could protect her and that a dead Raymond could no longer hurt her. How he could promise this— and Juli believe him— is beyond me. Waddard had never been able to protect himself from a living Raymond. He would hardly be able to protect Juli or himself from a dead Raymond.

"None of this—" Etta told her Crowner, the lift of her hand indicating the house in which they sat, "—none of what Waddard's success at the wheel provides for us, is worth what he's cost me and my daughter."

Faucon watched the bitter old woman as she took another sip of ale. No wonder guilt ate at Aldo. He'd not only left a boy locked in the prison of his mother's selfish love, but let Dickie suffer unkindness at the hands of even his own grandmother.

"If only Aldo had succeeded in trapping that corpse," Etta muttered with a sigh. "Then we could have dismembered Raymond and returned him forever to the earth, to rot as he deserves. Had we done that, my Juliana might have had a chance to live a real life."

"Tell me this, goodwife," Faucon said, not caring to share with her his offer to hunt down Raymond. "What, if anything, did you see on the road last night?"

"Nothing save for Raymond," Etta replied. "Or rather I heard Raymond. He's usually loudest down here, near the church. I didn't bother peering through the shutters as he passed."

"But you have seen him. What does he look like?" Alf wanted to know as he brought the skewer and toasted bread back to the table. The already dark bread now looked blackened. Here and there the melted lard glistened in the firelight. Sliding a slice in Faucon's direction, he took one for himself, then offered the third to Etta.

That had her shaking her head and pushing the slice back toward the middle of the table. "Split it between you two," she told Alf, before continuing. "He looks like a man wearing a dark tunic and swathed in a ragged cloak with a hood over his head.

"Raymond was hanged," she informed her guests, "and it's the hangman's hood he wears, proof of his sin and shameful death."

Faucon broke a piece from his slice and put it in his mouth. Usually, eating bread this dark was like chewing unmilled grain. But Etta's bread was surprisingly light and more flavorful than he expected, made all the more tasty saturated with rich, salted lard and crisped by the fire.

"Your mother taught you well," he said to Alf.

His man smiled at that. "So she did, sir."

Faucon looked at Etta. "How often do you see Raymond?"

"This past year he's reached the church door at least one time every two weeks. But there was a month when he came this far two times a week, for four or five weeks in a row. I vow to you. It's Juliana he follows. He trails her on the days my daughter goes to our church to make her confession."

That had Faucon eying the woman in surprise. "Every time he appears on your track it's on the same day your daughter visits your priest?"

She frowned at that. "Well, perhaps not every time, but more times than not it is the same night.

He swallowed his next bite of toast too quickly, cheating himself of savoring it, so he could speak. "Do you mean to say that Juliana goes to her confession after nightfall? But I thought none of you entered your church after dark."

"We don't," Etta told him firmly. "How can we with Raymond lurking at the church door, waiting to step inside? Nay, Juli prefers to make her confession later in the day. After that, she stops to visit with me on her way home. There are times when I have tasks I can't do alone, and she'll stay to help me with them. If Raymond is on the track before those chores are complete, Juli spends the night. This despite Waddard's protests that he and his children are now her family, and need her more than I do.

"As if she doesn't still need me, her own mother," Etta complained. "Hasn't she needed me more than ever this past year? Worry over Dickie has ground at my daughter until she's naught but bits and pieces. She's crumbling under the weight of caring for him, and all those other babies, while still working at the wheel to help Waddard put yet more silver in his coffers. And now with Waddard's hip, she must spend even more time at the wheel! I tell you, there are days when she's crying one instant and laughing like a madwoman in the next.

"But she's always better after a night here." Etta glanced from Alf to Faucon. "That's because I allow her to spew her rightful hatred of Raymond. Waddard won't allow her to speak his name in their home. He says it upsets the girls. How can he forbid Juli from bemoaning what's happening to her when Raymond's corpse is forever chasing after her, seeking her death?"

When the old woman continued, her voice was hard. "Waddard and Raymond are no different, not to my eyes. If

Raymond seeks to destroy Juli, thus cheating me of her, Waddard seeks to cheat Juli of her mother's love. Separating us is why he moved me here to this widow's cottage. Well, they've both failed. It's sweet satisfaction that Raymond's evil visitations have meant my daughter and I see far more of each other these days."

"Then Juliana was with you last night?" Faucon asked.

"Did I not just tell you Raymond was on the roadway last night?" Etta retorted sarcastically with a disbelieving shake of her head. "Of course she was here."

"And you both slept through the whole night, despite Raymond's moans?" he asked.

"Aye, doing so right there, in yon bed where Juliana now lies."

"Were you asleep by the time Raymond made his way to the church?" Faucon asked, shuffling his pieces in his head as he spoke.

"Juli was," Etta said. "My poor, sweet girl was no less distraught last night than she had been two days ago. She was yet fretting terribly over the damage Dickie had done to Aldo's house and what it would cost her and Waddard. As she cried, she cursed Raymond, both the man and the corpse, for all the evil he'd brought to her life. Raymond hadn't yet reached the church when I gave her a cup of elderberry wine and put her to bed. It was the same thing I'd done for her when she was yet a little lass, and too frightened to sleep." Tears filled her eyes.

"Can you say about what time Raymond returned past your window after he left the church? Was it closer to nightfall or midnight?" he asked, remembering Heyward's lesson.

Etta scrubbed away grief one more time, then her lips lifted in a hard, tight smile. "Neither. It was closer to overhearing Bett and Tibby argue."

Faucon's brows rose at that. "Why were they arguing?"

"Why else? Tibby's lack of a maidenhead and how Bett would never allow her daughter to wed with my grandson."

Etta shook her head in disgust. "That Bett! She's not just

a whore, but a rude whore. Despite that she knew full well Juli was within sound of her bold voice, she sent her curses and complaints about Dickie flying at the top of her lungs. She was so loud she stirred me from my dozing. I was grateful that Juli didn't awaken to hear her."

"Where was Raymond while they were arguing?"

"Moving up the track in the direction of Aldo's house. Where exactly I cannot say," Etta told him. "Let me tell you, it surprised me to hear Bett's door slam as their fight ended. As Bett walked away, she screamed that Tibby had best stay home or pay the price."

Faucon waited. When Etta added no more to what she'd said, he asked, "What was odd about that?"

Etta looked at him in surprise. "Well, Bett's the same as the rest of us, not wishing to meet Raymond on the track. It's because of Raymond that she usually leaves for Aldo's just before twilight, returning home on Aldo's arm long after that corpse has gone to wherever it goes to sleep."

Then the old woman's lip curled. "It's bad enough that Bett leaves her children alone when she goes to satisfy her lust. But to risk meeting Raymond and lose both life and soul, leaving them orphans with no hope of seeing her again in heaven?"

She spat out her disgust, then her expression softened. "It was a funny thing though. Bett's shouting hadn't disturbed Juliana, but when Bett slammed her door, my daughter came upright in the bed next to me. Although Juli was yet lost in her dreams, she asked me who had just come in, speaking to me as clear as day.

"I couldn't help myself," Etta said with a little laugh. "I told her that no one had come to visit us, that it was just Bett going to Aldo's to meet Raymond and so that corpse could finish her life. Then I drew her back down under the blanket. With my arms tight around my precious girl, I rocked us both to sleep."

"And after that you both slept without stirring all through

the night?" Faucon wanted to know.

"We did." Etta assured him.

"Not even rising to use the latrine?" Faucon pressed.

That had the old woman blinking in confusion. "Why does that matter? But if you must know, I didn't rise or even stir until gray light. Juli could only have done the same for when I awoke she was yet in the same place she'd been when I joined her in the bed. How that pleased me. I think that was the first time she'd had a full and peaceful night's sleep in a long while.

"She still slept when I left her to feed the fire. Much to my surprise, I heard Bett scratching at her door, calling softly for Tibby to open it. It seems she, too, had slept most of the night, albeit in the wrong bed."

Then Etta sighed heavily. "That was the last bit of normal in my day. The sun had only just appeared above the horizon when Father Godin arrived from Waddard's house with the news that Dickie was dead and his corpse rested in our church."

Again, her lip curled. "That coward, Waddard. He didn't even have the courage to come with our priest and to tell her himself."

Chapter Thirteen

aucon looked at Alf. "Finish your bread and ale. It's time we returned to the church. The vigil has begun and we must be ready against the possibility Dickie will rise."

"As you will, sir," Alf replied and hurried his last bites before gathering up their saddlebags.

"Thank you again, goodwife," Faucon told Etta as he came to his feet. "Both for this," he raised his last bite of toast in salute, "and for your help. If your daughter again seeks to run while yet trapped in her sleep, do you have some way to stop her?" he asked before putting that last piece into his mouth.

"Why would she run from me, her own mother?" Etta replied in surprise.

Faucon nodded at that. "Then I wish you and your daughter yet another quiet, restful night. However, should she escape you, you can come for me at the church. I'll help you search for her," he promised, then hurried back through the narrow passageway and out the door with Alf close behind him.

"That was abrupt," Alf said quietly as Etta barred her door behind them. "I take it she gave you whatever you sought?"

Faucon stepped down into the track. "She did," he nodded. Indeed, Etta had offered him many interesting pieces, but he'd found a place for only one thus far. Thankfully, it was the one he needed this very moment.

"Although I cannot yet prove it, I'm now certain that Raymond doesn't walk this track. Or rather, although Raymond's corpse may have once walked here, the one who has been walking the track for the past year is not Raymond," he amended.

In the dark Faucon more felt than saw Alf's confusion.

"But how can you say that when so many have witnessed him? Milo, the man who stabled our horses, told me the same as Etta said, that the corpse appears often on the track. Who is it they see if not Raymond?"

"They saw Dickie," Faucon told him. "That boy has been playing the role of his father, doing so to strike back at those here who scorned and disliked him. And he hasn't been doing it without help."

Across the track, the shutter covering Bett's front window was outlined by a rectangle of escaping light. If fire was strong enough to do that, someone was yet up and about. Signaling for Alf to follow, he started to Bett's door. "I intend to enter even if she refuses to allow me within," he warned as he went.

"You will break the door?" his man asked in surprise.

"I doubt I'll have to do that," Faucon assured him. He guessed Bett would open the door for him for no other reason than she knew he'd been with Etta. Aldo's paramour would want the chance to discover whatever the old woman might have said about her.

"Goodwife, it's Sir Faucon de Ramis," he announced as he knocked. "I must speak with you about Dickie."

Just as he expected, the door opened a short moment later. Bett held a small clay bowl in her hand, a tallow lamp. Its flame danced wildly as air streamed from the outside in, drawn by her fire. She yet wore her close-fitting brown gown, but in the privacy of her own home she'd removed her head covering and loosened her black hair. It hung in waves to near her waist.

Faucon looked past her. Her house had the same design as Etta's, with a narrow passageway that cut it in twain. Now, between light from Bett's fire streaming through the leftward opening at the end of the passage and her lamp, he made sense of the layout. The house had two sides, one where the humans lived and the other given over to animals, at least during the depths of winter. Shutters covered long openings in both sides of the passageway. When they were raised, the heat of the stabled animals would join that of the fire, helping to warm the house during the coldest months.

"Huh, have you come to tell me that you were wrong to stop me from what I intended, that the boy tries to walk?" the pretty woman asked rudely.

"He hasn't yet, but if he does, he won't get far," Faucon replied, thinking it a shame that a woman with such a lovely face would be so ugly at her core. "He's bound and blinded, and being watched by six of your neighbors. You and your daughter need not worry."

"God be praised for small miracles," Bett retorted harshly.

Faucon placed his foot on her threshold. "I know it's late but as you heard me say at the church, I'm tasked with finding the one who killed Dickie."

"Raymond killed that rogue," Bett snapped back.

"So I've been told," Faucon agreed. "However, I'd like to speak to your daughter about the boy. I heard your charge on the track, that she and Dickie have been trysting. It seems they were seeking their pleasure on the same nights that you visited Aldo's bed," he added boldly.

Shock flattened Bett's expression. Then her eyes narrowed. She looked across the track at Etta's house. "That jealous old telltale. Whatever she said, you can be sure it was a lie."

"Does Aldo also lie?" Faucon asked, now putting his hand on her door, pressing it back against the passageway wall.

Bett caught a swift breath at the news of her lover's betrayal. Faucon brought his other foot up to the threshold, thus preventing her from closing the door. Startled, she stepped back from him.

"Hey now. I didn't invite you to enter. You'll return outside this moment," she demanded, once again plying a forceful manner, seeking to intimidate a man into doing her will.

Faucon pressed his shoulder to her door, pinning it in place. "My man and I won't stay long. There are a few things I don't understand about Dickie's death, and I believe Tibby can help me make sense of them."

As if drawn to it by the sound of her name on a stranger's

tongue, Bett's daughter stepped halfway out of the opening at the end of the passageway. Framed by light from the fire, he could see that grief yet stained the pretty girl's face. Eyes wide, Tibby stared at him as she nipped at her lower lip.

"Will you speak to me of Dickie and the trick the two of you have been playing on your neighbors this last year?" he asked the girl.

For an instant shock kept the girl frozen where she stood. Then panic flashed across Tibby's face. With a tiny squeak, she exploded into motion. Hems flying, she leapt across the passageway and into the stable. Thinking she meant to flee the house, Faucon shoved past Bett and followed.

"Nay! Stop you! You have no right," Bett shouted after him.

An instant later she cried, "Hey you, leave go of me," suggesting Alf now restrained her.

Faucon turned into the stable entrance and stopped short. A half-door, meant to prevent the animals from moving into living area, blocked his path. Beyond it, the stable was dark and cool. And still. The air was scented with hints of last year's manure and the sweet-sharp smell of rotted straw.

Peering into the dimness, he identified two stalls directly ahead of him. Each had a chest-high withe panel for a door. Between him and the stalls a double door cut into the back wall. No doubt it opened up into the toft, allowing the owner to move animals in and out as needed.

With that, another piece fell into place. If Waddard's home was the same as this one, this door was how Dickie escaped without his parents noting. He'd only needed to creep into the stable and use this door, leaving it unbarred behind him.

Right now, Bett's stable door was not only closed but barred. Tibby was still here. Opening the half-door, he stepped inside, the thick layer of straw muffling his footsteps.

He stopped and closed his eyes. Filtering out Bett's continuing curses and demands that Alf release her, he caught the sound of rustling. It came from the darker of the two stalls, the one filled at its back with a dark mound. That could only be hay, fodder for the winter.

Its door was slightly ajar. Cloaked in shadows, her back to him, Tibby knelt in front of the haystack. The movement of her arms said she pushed something deep into that loose pile, doing her best to make no sound as she worked.

Stepping inside, Faucon pulled the door closed behind him, in case the girl thought to run, and stopped a few feet behind her. Tibby shot a swift glance over her shoulder then freed a wild cry. She leapt to her feet, her hands clasped at her heart.

"Mama?!" she cried, sounding panicked.

"Tibby! What are you doing to my daughter?" came Bett's frightened response. "Let me go, let me go," she begged of Alf this time.

In the stall, Tibby put her hands on her hips and drew herself up in a parody of her mother's bold manner. "Go away! Leave me alone!"

"Oh lass, it's too late for that," Faucon told her. "I know what you and Dickie were doing when you weren't trysting. I also know what you put into that pile."

That was all it took. Tibby's false courage drained from her. Even in the dimness Faucon could see her chin began to quiver. He closed his hand around one of her wrists. She yelped but didn't resist. Then, shoulders shaking, she began to weep.

"Alf, I need you in here," Faucon called.

"Nay, you have no right to enter! Stop, stop I say!" Bett cried helplessly, her protests marking Alf's passage toward the stable.

Alf entered with Bett directly behind him. She'd wrapped her free hand in his belt, doing her best to stop him while carrying the yet-burning lamp in her other hand. When Alf opened the stall door, Bett pushed herself away from him, stumbling to a halt at the wall between the two stalls.

"Dastard!" she chided Faucon. "You have no right to be in my home, nor have you the right to touch my daughter. You'll let her go and leave!"

"Hold the girl for me," Faucon commanded Alf.

Lips trembling and her tears yet flowing, Tibby meekly allowed Alf to close his hand around her upper arm. Faucon went to kneel at the front of the stack. Thrusting his hands into it, he sifted through the loosely stacked straw. Its sweet, green smell filled the air, a reminder of the summer just past.

Tibby hadn't had time enough to do a proper job of hiding them. Faucon pulled out a length of tattered fabric. Leaving it on the ground in front of him, he again reached into the straw. There was no mistaking the way the flake of dried blood. This time, he brought forth the hood that had prevented Dickie from seeing his assailant. It was rolled around a dark-colored tunic that was also filthy with dried blood.

Gathering the garments in his arms, he returned to his feet. A handsome, black-haired boy of no more eight now clung to the jamb of the stable doorway. Dressed only in a blanket, his curling hair sleep-tossed and his eyes heavy-lidded, he stared at Faucon, wide-eyed.

Faucon shook out the tattered cloak, holding it up for all to see. Tibby's sobs became hiccoughs. She turned her face to the side as if she couldn't bear to look upon the proof of her sin.

Bett's mouth opened in shock as she recognized the garment. "Nay, that cannot be!" Then the woman grimaced in revulsion. "That thing— that thing cannot be here!"

"That's not all I found," Faucon said. Draping the cloak over his arm, he showed Tibby's mother the bloodied tunic and hood.

Bett moaned then crossed herself. "Get those away from us," she pleaded, sounding as terrified of the clothing as she was of the one she believed had worn them.

"If I search a little longer will I find Dickie's garments and his shoes?" Faucon asked the girl.

Tibby began to tremble. Her knees gave way. As she sank to kneel on the ground, Alf released her.

She stared at the straw in front of her as she spoke. "They

weren't anywhere in the smithy when I found him."

"Should they have been?" he asked her.

She gave a watery nod. "When he— his garments would have been in a sack. When he walked, he carried them with him on his back, hidden under his cloak. They—" A sob overtook her and she fell silent.

"Where in the smithy did you find the cloak and hood?" Faucon wanted to know.

Tibby gasped for a moment, her body almost convulsing, as she fought to catch her breath. "The hood he yet wore. His cloak was laid to one side," she whimpered without looking up.

Faucon nodded as another piece slipped into place. "And where was he when you found him?"

Still watching her feet, she gagged a little. "He was on his belly on the smithy floor. He was still bleeding," she moaned.

Raising her watery gaze to look at him, Tibby struggled to speak. Her mouth quivered so badly her words were hard to understand. "I— had to drag him to the anvil," she gasped out. "I was crying so that I could hardly see. But I had to take those—" she pointed to the garments he held. "I had to. I didn't want anyone to know what he'd— what we'd— done."

She dragged in a breath. "It was so hard. I sat him up so I could—" She sobbed soundlessly for a moment.

"There was so much blood," she cried. Extending her hands, she turned them palms up and stared into them. By the light of her mother's lamp, Faucon could see the brownish stains her sweetheart's blood had left upon her flesh. "When I pulled off the hood, it smeared across his face. I didn't want to leave him— I tried to clean away some— but I only made it worse."

"Was the smithy always where he began and ended his walk?"

She shook her head at that.

"Then where?" Faucon wanted to know.

"In the west field," she managed. "That's where everyone said Raymond appeared and disappeared."

"Then why was he in the smithy last night?" Faucon asked.

Again, Tibby's sobs cheated her of breath. "Dickie was so angry at Aldo for sending him away when he'd done no wrong. He said we needed to find some way to shame him. We were going to—" her voice trailed into silence.

She tried again. "We were going to—" She turned her head to the side, buried her face in her hands and gave a tiny, horrified cry.

"You were going to tryst there," Faucon said for her. Taking Tibby in Aldo's shop would have been Dickie's way of biting his thumb at his uncle, even if Aldo never learned what they'd done.

"I don't understand any of this," Bett cried, her voice pitched somewhere between heartbreak and panic. "What are those things doing in my home? How is it you have them, Tibby?"

When Tibby didn't lift her head from her hands to answer, Faucon asked the girl, "Will you not explain to your mother how you and Dickie have been hoodwinking her and your neighbors?" His voice was softer than she deserved. But then, what came next for her would likely be a torment worthy of hell.

Tibby's only response was another tiny horrified cry.

Faucon looked at Bett. "Not only has your daughter been trysting with Dickie, but she's been helping Dickie play the role of Raymond in your track."

Bett's mouth opened. Her eyes widened. As she understood the full meaning of what he'd said, her face whitened with something akin to terror. She sagged against the wall, trembling. Alf took her lamp from her, to prevent yet another catastrophe.

"Tibby, how could you?" Bett cried, sounding as frightened as she looked. "When the others learn what you've done, the whole village will rise up against us. We'll be fortunate if even one soul ever speaks to us again. God save us all!" Bett turned her plea for heavenly intervention into a horrified gasp. "What if they banish us? What will we do if they drive us away? How will we live?"

Faucon reached down and closed his hand around Tibby's upper arm. When he tugged, she came to her feet without resisting, her face yet hidden in her hands.

"Goodwife," he said to Bett, "I'm taking your daughter to the church with me. Your reeve and the others who hold vigil over Dickie's body must be told what she and he have been doing."

When Bett began to weep, it was in great gusting sobs that Etta no doubt heard from across the track.

Chapter Fourteen

"**B**ut that isn't possible," Heyward protested, his voice rising to a pained note.

Holding the tattered cloak out in front of him, the blood-stained brown tunic and hood draped over his arms, Faucon stood in the nave, a few steps closer to the altar than Tibby. The moment that the girl caught sight of her dead love, hooded and bound, against the back wall, she'd refused to come any farther into the church. Faucon had granted her that much, but left Alf with her to see that she stayed where she stood.

Tibby once more had her hands clutched at her heart. Every line of her body said facing the hangman would be less fearsome than what she was now being asked to do. Bett had been wrong. The dead Dickie hadn't needed to walk to steal Tibby's soul.

As for Bett, she stood a little behind her daughter and Alf. Although she'd snatched her headcloth before leaving her home, tying it around her head as they walked, her hair yet flowed free around her. Slow tears made their way down the woman's cheeks, dropping unheeded onto the breast of her gown. Yet wrapped in his blanket, her son clung close to her, his arms around her waist, his head pressed against her arm.

"Heyward, look at the garments," Watt told the old man, a sharp edge to his voice. "They are exactly what they appear to be, Raymond's attire." The heavyset man folded his arms as he spoke. In his upset he forgot he held a cup in one hand. Plum wine dribbled onto the floor as it tilted.

"I can only agree with Watt," Aldo said, glancing at his neighbors. "These are Raymond's garments. Haven't we all seen him wear them when he walks?" Repressed anger made his words hard.

The moment Aldo understood why Faucon brought his paramour and her family to the church, he'd backed away until there was a good distance between them. Bett was right to worry over how she and her children might be punished for Tibby's misdeed.

"It looks like Raymond's cloak, and his hood and tunic," Gervis agreed reluctantly.

"Is that why Dickie died, because he stole Raymond's garments from him?" Tom suggested tenuously, his brow creased. "But if Raymond killed Dickie for that theft, then why did he leave his garments behind after Dickie was dead?"

Faucon wasn't certain if he wanted to laugh or shake his head in disbelief. Godin was right. These folk were wedded to the very idea of Raymond on their track. It would be hard for them to let that go.

"These garments never belonged to Raymond," Faucon said to Tom, his words meant for all the men in the church.

He looked at Tibby. "Where did you and Dickie get them?"

Head still bowed, the girl drew a broken breath. It took her a moment to push the words off her tongue. "From the merchants who passed by our doors. Dickie used Goodman Waddard's silver—"

Although her mouth continued to move, she made no sound. She gasped. Her nose reddened as another round of tears began to dribble down her face. When she again opened her mouth, words exploded out in a rush.

"It wasn't just Dickie. It was all of us. Dickie only played Raymond some of the time. When he couldn't win free for the night, Will, Rob, or Matty—" As she offered these names, she looked from Gervis to Bertie and then to Watt, "—would play the role in his place. Whoever knew he could escape his home that night would be Raymond."

Faucon's brows rose. The meaning of Godin's cryptic words suddenly became clear. So too did he see why Jilly hadn't been frightened to walk the track at night. It seemed Raymond's true identity had been a closely-guarded secret among some of Mancetter's children.

The fathers of the three named lads swayed in unwelcome surprise. Watt dropped his wooden cup. It skittered away from him on the slick tile. "By God, I'll have his hide for sure," he snarled, and started for the door.

"Stop, Watt," Aldo commanded.

Watt stopped. His fists clenched. Bright color flushed his face. "Do you dare try to prevent me from punishing my own son?" he shouted at his reeve.

"Of course not," Aldo retorted, holding his hands out in a gesture of peace. "He's your son. But there's something important you must hear, really hear, before you leave."

Aldo looked at Faucon. "My mind is clear now. Tell them and make them accept it as you have done for me."

Faucon glanced from man to man, then let his gaze come to rest on Watt. "Think on it," he urged the raging father. "If what Tibby says is true, and it was Dickie's turn to play the role of Raymond last night, it couldn't have been Raymond who killed him, not unless Dickie killed himself, which I'm absolutely certain he did not. So if that much is true, who among you killed that boy?" He pointed toward Dickie's corpse as he continued. "For it could only have been one of your neighbors who did this deed."

Watt's hands opened. His eyes widened as the anger drained from his face. "Holy Mother, save me," he breathed in prayer. "Sir, I didn't mean it when I said I'd considered killing Dickie. He isn't dead because of me, you must believe me!" he cried, in more plea than protest.

"Nay, it cannot have been any of us," Heyward said, the former certainty in his voice now shredded by doubt and not a little shock. "How could it be? We all know that Raymond promised to kill Juliana and his own son. Didn't he return when Waddard wed Juliana just as he'd vowed to do? Didn't he nearly break down Waddard's door, trying to reach her and Dickie so he could do the deed? Nay, it can only have been Raymond! None of us would have done such a thing," he strove again to insist. Instead, his voice trailed off into an uncertain silence.

Bertie shook his head as one stunned. "This cannot be true. We've all seen Raymond time and again. How could we look at him and not have recognized one of our own boys?" He sounded as lost as Heyward. "But what of that time Raymond disappeared right before our eyes while we chased him. We all saw it, didn't we Gervis? How could any of our boys have done that?"

That had Gervis nodding. "You're right, no living soul can do that."

Faucon looked at Tibby. She now visibly trembled. He wondered if she might faint. "Do you know anything about this?" he asked her.

"That was Will," she replied with the tiniest of nods, her voice quivering along with her limbs. As she said that, she lifted her head and her gaze flickered to Gervis before returning to the floor. "He said that the three of you drew so close he feared being caught. So he ceased to move as Raymond, and instead hurried ahead. He said he was so frightened it felt as if his heart might explode from his chest. When he thought he was far enough, he fell forward between the rows and pressed flat against the earth. You had all stopped some way behind him, looking to see where he'd gone. As you walked in circles, he crawled ahead in the row. There he stayed until you left the field."

Gervis's expression could have been carved from stone. "He crawled like the worm he is," he muttered.

Beside him, Bertie turned his back on the girl. "I can't hear any more of this. I'm going home."

"But the vigil," Heyward cried in worry. "Dickie must be watched."

Gervis only shook his head and went to take one of the torches he'd left at the back wall. "You'll have to watch him without us," he said, lifting it to the flaming brand on the wall above him. As it flared into new life, he turned toward the door. Bertie joined him.

"I'll walk with you," Watt said and the three started across the nave. None of them glanced at Tibby as they passed her.

"But what of Dickie?" Heyward protested again, throwing his cry at the backs of his departing neighbors. "Who will stop him if he rises?"

"I'll yet be here," Faucon replied, offering the old man a reassuring nod. Just then the sacristy door squeaked open and Brother Edmund entered. Faucon's nod to the monk encouraged Edmund to join him. "And as you can see, my clerk and my man are here as well.

"What of you, Tom?" Faucon asked of the slight man. "Will you also stay?"

Tom, whose daughter was too young to have participated in this youthful mummery, shrugged at that. "I told my wife I wouldn't be back before dawn. If I knock on the door now, it might frighten her. I may as well stay."

"As will I," Aldo said, his tone flat. He looked at his paramour. "Take your daughter home, Bett."

"Aldo?" Bett filled his name with all her shattered hopes for their future.

"Not now," was all he said.

With a noisy gasp, Bett grabbed Tibby by the hand. Pulling her daughter around with her, she started after the departing men, moving slowly so she kept well back from them. Her shoulders shook, saying she cried. Her son followed close behind her, yet holding a fold of her gown skirt as if he feared he might lose her.

As Alf and Brother Edmund came to stand with Faucon, the monk frowned as he watched Bett's boy close the church door behind him. "Where do they all go?" he asked. "I thought they meant to spend the night."

"So they did, but circumstances have changed," Faucon replied, as Tom and Heyward retreated to the pile of hay. Two of the three jugs of wine had been opened in his absence.

Tom's sack was now spread on the floor near the pile. Placed atop it was a small wheel of golden cheese and a few sausages. Faucon wondered if the ruin of an enjoyable evening— at least for the men who'd come for the vigil— would be another thing for which Mancetter's folk blamed Dickie.

"And the reeve also intends to stay," Faucon added as Aldo joined them.

He offered the smith an apologetic smile as he began to bundle the garments draped over his arms into the cloak. "Would that I'd found something other than I have," he said, speaking to Aldo in French this time.

Although the corners of Aldo's mouth rose, a soul-deep sadness filled his eyes. "You found what I would never have seen, even if I'd found it. I will have much to account for on the day I meet our Lord, I think," he said, proving himself competent in the tongue of the nobles. "I, more than all the rest, should have realized. Why couldn't I see?"

"You saw what you expected to see, just as the boys intended," Faucon replied.

That had Brother Edmund eying them in surprise. "What did he expect to see?"

"There was no corpse walking Mancetter's track nor was Dickie killed by his dead father," Faucon told him. "Raymond's appearance on their lane was in fact a mummery, a prank played by a group of village lads, Dickie among them. The boys took turns wearing these garments—" He raised the bundled clothing. "—as they pretended to be the dead man. It was Dickie's turn to play his dead sire last night."

As Faucon said that, a strange thought hit him. If it had been another boy's turn, would he have died in Dickie's place? But another boy wouldn't have been in the smithy, meeting Tibby. Aldo was right. It had simply been the boy's time.

Outrage, rather than the disappointment Faucon expected, flared red on Brother Edmund's pale face. "That is no prank," the monk cried. "To pretend to be such an evil creature is to invite Satan into your soul. Those boys deserve a heavy penance, not just to cleanse them of wrongdoing, but to protect them from the Devil's eye!"

"I suspect the Devil is the least of those boys' worries at the moment," Alf murmured, then looked at Aldo. "I see three jugs over there. What do you say I help you drown your guilt with whatever they contain?"

Aldo managed something that passed for a laugh. "What else have I to do tonight?"

As the two former soldiers went to join Heyward and Tom, Brother Edmund looked at his employer. "What happened to the boy's mother? Did she at last rouse and go home?"

"Of a sort," Faucon replied. "She tried to stop her neighbors as they were binding her son. When she failed, she ran from the church. I caught her and took her to her mother's home."

"So, if Raymond didn't kill the boy, who did?" Edmund wanted to know.

"The one who took the boy's shoes and garments from him after he was dead," Faucon replied, leaning down to tuck the bundle of Raymond's attire under the corner of the altar. Given what they represented, he wondered if they shouldn't be burned. As Brother Edmund had said, they were an invitation to evil.

"Ah," Brother Edmund said in acknowledgment. Then the disappointment Faucon had expected a moment earlier now crept across the monk's face. "You realize that there's no longer a need for a vigil. That is, assuming it's true the boy had no contact with a walking corpse."

"So I suspected," Faucon replied, nodding. "But there's no sense in spoiling the evening any more than it's already been spoiled by Raymond's abrupt and unexpected disappearance from Mancetter."

The monk sighed. "Shame on me. As sinful as it is, I would have liked to have seen a corpse afoot. Not even Master Walter has witnessed that. For shame on me saying so. I know better than most that nothing good ever comes from such an encounter. Of those who survive an encounter, most usually perish soon after. Crops fail. Animals die."

"If it helps, I'll admit to wishing the same," Faucon said, as his own disappointment rose. What should have been a thrilling hunt had in fact become far more painful than he could have imagined. He sighed and set aside that thought.

"What say you? Now that your prayers are complete, there's a tray of foods from Father Godin on the dais, as well as what those men brought with them. Join us," Faucon invited his clerk.

Edmund's shrug was a stiff lift of his shoulders. His mouth curved upward into that tight-lipped smile of his. "All I can do is echo what the reeve said. What else have I to do?" Then he grumbled, "Save pass the hours watching a corpse that will not walk."

It didn't take long before Heyward had encouraged Alf and Aldo to share tales of their adventures in foreign lands with strange customs to pass the time. Unable to follow the conversation, and likely with no interest in the subject, Brother Edmund had piled a layer of hay between him and the cold tile floor, then curled onto it. His back was to the sanctuary and his cloak wrapped tightly around him. He'd pulled his cowl over his eyes.

Seated near Dickie, his back to the wall, Faucon took another sip of the plum wine. Brother Augustine wasn't the only man in this hundred who could craft a fine brew. That said, Faucon thought it unlikely that the monk's perry offered the same outcome that this wine would. Overindulging guaranteed a headache come the dawn.

With that thought, he remembered that Will yet slept in the priest's house. Or so Faucon hoped. He glanced at the torches on the wall. They were beginning to sputter. It wouldn't be long before they burned out, and the one Gervis had left behind was used as a replacement. Against the possibility that he might need a torch to search for his brother, Faucon set aside his cup and came to his feet.

Alf broke off in the middle of his description of a Saracen temple. "Sir?"

"Stay," Faucon told his man, as he pulled his cloak around him. "I'm going to see that my brother is settled for the night. He sleeps in the priest's house."

That had Alf, who understood what plagued Will, frowning in concern. "If you need me—"

"I'll fetch you," Faucon finished with a grateful nod.

As Faucon entered the sacristy, he glanced around him. It was truly no more than a lean-to, holding several chests and a medium-sized coffer. Neither the bar nor the outside door, nor the walls of the lean-to, for that matter, was strong enough to stop a determined invader. That Mancetter's folk hadn't broken into their church this way to reach Dickie said something about their respect for their Lord's house, if not their priest.

Outside the door, the night was cold but not bitter. A dog barked. The eerie screech of a barn owl echoed in the distance. Nothing moaned or moved on the track.

With the moon settling toward the western horizon, the sky overhead was alive with stars. It was by their light that Faucon found his way around the church in search of the priest's house. He couldn't have missed it, for it stood only a few short feet behind the east end of the church.

It looked no different than the rest of the homes in this village, with a door at the middle of the front wall and a thatch roof. The smoke swirling up out of the roof was thick enough to block out the stars. Bright firelight outlined the closed shutter in the front wall.

Although no man left a fire that strong untended, Faucon knocked with no confidence that he'd receive an answer. Much to his relief, a man called, "Come." Since the voice didn't belong to either Godin or Will, this must be Father Berold.

He was surprised to find the door unbarred. This, when Raymond was said to have rattled this very latch. One more time, he made his way up the narrow passageway that separated these homes.

The living area looked much the same as Etta's room, with a central hearth, benches and table at one side, foodstuffs at the other wall, as well as hanging from the rafters. But here, a prie-dieu had been pushed against the wall next to the opening to the passageway. There were two beds placed against the far wall.

The one in the corner had woolen drapes hanging from poles attached to the ceiling. The draperies were presently open, revealing that the bed they were meant to surround was nothing but a narrow pallet on the floor. It was empty, the blanket that covered it neatly tucked around it.

The other bed stood in the same place as Etta's. Like hers, it was just a hay-filled pallet, but this one was wide and long enough to accommodate more than two sleepers. Also like Etta's bed, this one had been laid atop a wooden frame that stood almost waist-high. Draperies also curtained this bed. Those on the long sides had been pulled shut, but the panel that would cover the foot was yet open, thus allowing the fire's heat to enter.

Will sprawled across the crude mattress. He wore his underarmor but not his boots. Faucon smiled. Just as when they'd shared a bed, his brother had kicked the blanket away until he could expose his bare feet to the air.

There was no sign of Godin or his wife but a man wrapped tightly in a thick blanket sat in the half-barrel chair placed close to the hearth. Father Berold, for it was surely he, wore his dark hair cropped close to his head. Heavily threaded with silver, his thick brows were straight lines over his sunken, pale eyes. His cheeks were gaunt and where shadows clung, Faucon saw death's inexorable approach.

Of a sudden, the priest's right arm burst free of his wrap. It rose upward. His hand fluttered. The man brought it back beneath the blanket, then his head twitched to the side and his shoulders jerked. One foot danced.

"You must be Sir Faucon," he said in English, his smile more grimace than grin.

Or so Faucon thought he said. As Godin had warned, Father Berold's words were oddly slurred.

The muscles at Berold's throat moved. Again he spoke. It took Faucon a moment to decipher the sounds as, "Brother Edmund says you are our new Coronarius and he serves you as clerk."

"You spoke with him?" Faucon asked, startled that this priest might be fluent in French.

Father Berold nodded. The skin of his cheek moving oddly. "But I'm easier to comprehend in my native tongue. Godin said you speak it."

"Ah," Faucon replied at that. "Have Godin and his wife departed?"

This time the man's left hand exited from beneath his blanket. Although his fingers wriggled, he managed to bring them to his face as if to wipe away a tear. His next words were even more garbled, as much by his tongue as by his emotions. Faucon caught *not wife, sister,* and *sad.*

That had Faucon glancing again at the smaller bed. His liking for Godin grew along with his respect. He regretted that he would never know their story.

"Come, sit," Father Berold invited. He turned his head in the direction of the table. Faucon followed his look to a stool. Setting it near the fire, he sat facing the priest.

"Dickie walks?" Berold asked.

"I think not," Faucon told him, beginning to catch the nuances of the man's odd pronunciation. "Dickie wasn't killed by Raymond. Brother Edmund says that if the boy didn't interact with the dead man, he's not likely to rise."

His head twitching, the priest frowned. "If not Raymond, then who?"

"I'm not certain yet," Faucon replied on a sigh, praying that his pieces would rearrange themselves yet once again. "Did you know Dickie was playing the part of Raymond on your track?"

What looked like surprise lifted the man's brows. "Holy Mother save him," he offered in swift prayer. Then he grimaced again. "But I must admit a clever trick. That boy! Too much wit. He was too big for this place."

"Dickie recruited other village lads to help him. Tibby, as well," Faucon said. "Brother Edmund warns that they'll need God's protection to ward off the evil they've called to them. With Father Godin gone, will you be able to offer them that?"

Again the man's brows lifted. "If their parents allow," he said. "Otherwise, they'll have to go— Atherstone."

Then Father Berold frowned. "Tibby as well? Bett must be beside herself."

"She is, fearing banishment," Faucon replied.

"Let her know," the priest said, then paused as another twitch overtook him. "She can be here. With me. I will need her help." Then, his hands and feet dancing, Father Berold said, "What of Juliana? Godin says she's— again that strange sleep of hers."

Faucon stared at the twitching man in surprise. "She's slept in this same way in the past?"

The priest's head moved up and down as if he nodded, although the movement was close enough to a twitch that Faucon wasn't certain. Faucon waited as Father Berold marshaled his words. This time when the priest spoke, Faucon deciphered the man's remarks with ease.

"More than once. After Raymond took her and they handfasted, she walked the lane. On and off. For about a year. Woe to anyone who woke her. A piercing scream."

"So I've heard for myself," Faucon said with a smile. "I take it you were here, then, when Raymond first appeared after his death?"

Again the afflicted man managed a nod. It ended in a leftward jerk of his head. "Saw him," he said, and tried to point to his eyes in demonstration.

"You're certain he was dead?"

That won Faucon a frown from the priest, one that

suggested uncertainty. "Was barely dawn. Still half-light. I'd left the shivaree earlier than the others. Awoke to Juliana and Waddard screaming. I ran. Most others slept. I saw Raymond. He looked like a man alive. For certain he acted as if— as he tore at Old Dickie's house. Other doors began to open."

Father Berold paused and gathered his breath. "That's when Raymond saw me."

Berold drew his hand from beneath his blanket. His fingers strained, his hand flapped. As he regained control of his limb, the priest made the same hand gesture that Godin had used. "He disappeared before my eyes. I so vow by all— holy. Not alive. Couldn't be." This last was more a question than a statement.

"I'm told he returned a few times after that before Dickie began his performance a year ago," Faucon said.

Father Berold either shrugged or twitched. "So others claim. I never saw him again. But for the year after Raymond's attack on her home, Juliana again walked in her sleep. Not even holy water helped. Perhaps Raymond had bewitched her?"

Again, the man offered that grimace. His feet tapped. There was definitely something wriggling in his cheek. Had it not been for Godin's warning, Faucon might well have run from this place, believing the man mad or possessed, or both.

"Strange to watch her like that. She seems so awake. Once she worked at the wheel. Hours. Waddard called me to witness. He feared the devil used her. I spoke the words to drive out evil and applied holy water."

He tried to shake his head but his shoulders twitched instead. "She kept working. Even spoke to us. But her eyes were—"

Again he paused, this time to swallow. "Wrong."

Faucon nodded in agreement. "That's what I saw just a short while ago when she ran from the church. I took her to her mother's home. Tell me this, if you can. How is it neither Juliana nor Waddard knew that Dickie was coming and going from their home during the night?"

"So many reasons. Too busy with their trade. Juliana too obsessed with Dickie to see him as he was. Waddard too determined to protect— Dickie from Raymond's legacy," Father Berold said then paused for a long breath. "But Jilly knew. It was she who came this morn, pounding on the door, calling for Father Godin."

Faucon sighed. Of course it was Jilly, the girl who had no fear of Raymond. His questions answered, he started to rise, then glanced at his sleeping brother. But to startle Will was to risk Will running from him.

"Does my brother's presence inconvenience you?" he asked the priest.

"Not at all," the twitching man replied.

Father Berold's face was still for an instant. This time the curve of his lips was natural, and filled with compassion. "I recognize a fellow sufferer. I have added him to my prayers."

Faucon eyed the priest for a long moment. Of such mettle were saints forged. "For that you have my eternal gratitude, Father."

Chapter Fifteen

Seated with his back to the wall and his legs outstretched, Faucon snapped out of his doze into full awareness. His right hand moved instinctively for the sword he wasn't wearing. He caught back his arm. The torches had died earlier, and the steady flow of air through the sanctuary had blown out the candle. He stared into the impenetrable darkness that again held the church in thrall, listening for what had startled him.

Hay rustled. That was Alf, rising to sitting. Another rustle marked Aldo as he also stirred from his sleep. Heyward snored to his right. There was no sound from either Tom or Brother Edmund.

Then Faucon caught it. It wasn't quite a rustle, nor exactly the scurrying of a rat. Although the sound lasted but a short instant, that was long enough for him to place it near Dickie.

A silent moment passed, then another. Just as Faucon began to relax, it came again. This time there was no question that it came from Dickie.

He shot to his feet. In a heartbeat, Alf and Aldo were with him. They arranged themselves in the dark around the hooded and bound boy.

"He moves?" Aldo whispered.

"So it seems," Faucon replied in the same low voice. Then he wondered why they were whispering. If Dickie sought to rise, they needed to awaken the others. Then his lips tightened over what must follow. Cutting the boy in pieces was no small task. More importantly, it was no task for a sword. What did it say that the men who had come to keep watch had brought wine and food, but no axe or a saw?

There was another soft, rasping scratch. Faucon blinked. Had Dickie's head just dropped closer to his knees? Without thinking, he extended a hand, meaning to test the boy for a reaction.

Just before his fingers reached Dickie's bare shoulder, he froze. What if this was how the dead began to move? What if Dickie already carried that sickness?

Again, the boy slid, this time shifting to the side a little. Daring much, Faucon placed his forefinger on the top of Dickie's head and gave the corpse a gentle push. That was all it took to send the boy's body slipping down to the floor. It came to rest on its side, Dickie's hooded head yet propped against the wall. And there he stayed.

Faucon freed a quiet bark of amusement. "He doesn't move, he only softens," he whispered to the others, relieved that he didn't need to raise his voice. "Brother Edmund was right. He won't walk because he never had any contact with a reanimated corpse. But he will be ready for washing and winding on the morrow."

Aldo sighed, his breath clouding in the chill air of the church. "I wonder if any man in Mancetter will have an ounce of pride remaining when all of this is said and done. To think we were haunted and hoodwinked by our own children."

Behind them, the nave door of the church creaked. All three men pivoted. The door scraped softly over the tiles until it stopped, only half-open. Silver starlight spilled in through the gap, outlining the darkened form of the one who entered. It was no man nor hooded walking corpse, just a slight woman. She cradled something in her arms. Skirt swinging, she started toward them.

"Juliana," Faucon whispered to Alf and Aldo. "I think she walks in her sleep. I want to see what she does. Come," he said, drawing them back to the sacristy door.

"God save me! Is she again walking in her sleep? It's been so long since she last did that I'd forgotten that about her," Aldo breathed.

"She walks while sleeping?" Alf whispered in sharp surprise. Both Faucon and Aldo hushed him.

If Juliana heard them, she gave no sign of it. As if it were as light as day, Dickie's mother rounded the corner of the altar, then knelt beside her son, her back to them. Enough starlight reached that wall to show Faucon that she wore no cloak and her feet were bare. Setting whatever she carried beside Dickie, the woman leaned toward the corpse and began to loosen the knots that kept him bound. Once Juliana had freed Dickie of his bindings, she wrestled the hood from his head, then reached out to stroke her son's cheek.

"What is this? Do you yet sleep?" she asked of her dead boy. "But it's time for you to rise."

She paused, still and quiet, as if she listened to Dickie's reply. The possibility that she might actually be hearing something sent a shiver up Faucon's spine.

"But of course you're cold as ice," she said in response to nothing. "You left without your clothing. And your shoes, you foolish lad! What sort of clodpate goes about without his shoes this time of year? See here, I have them for you." As she spoke, Juliana opened the sack and pulled out Dickie's tunic, then his shoes.

Faucon bowed his head. There was no satisfaction in seeing proof of what his pieces had already told him.

"Sir," Alf said, definitely sounding unnerved this time, "how can she have his shoes unless she was in the smithy before the girl?"

"And so she was," Faucon replied sadly, "sent there in her sleep by her own mother's sarcastic comment."

There, in the smithy, Juliana had come upon 'Raymond,' cloaked and hooded. Lost in her strange sleep, she'd done the one thing that she must have longed to do from the day Raymond had taken her. She'd used Aldo's hammer to put an end to the evil that had befouled her life.

"Now we'll have to get you dressed. You're right, that will be quite a chore. You're no longer a little lad, are you?" she was telling the corpse.

All three men stayed where they stood, watching as she dressed her son. When Juliana was done, she curled up next to Dickie and returned to wherever it was that her strange sleep took her.

Rather than sleep, Faucon sat near Juliana for the rest of the night. It wasn't to keep watch over her. He had no doubt she'd remain where she was until she finally awakened. It was he who wouldn't be able to sleep.

Instead, he spent the next few hours turning and rearranging those pieces of his, praying that there might be something he'd missed. Nothing changed, not the sequence of events nor the name he would have to announce to the jury. When he at last admitted defeat, he turned his gaze to the half-open door to watch as night slowly gave way to day.

When the sky was tinted pink, he rose and went to kneel next to Juliana. He took her hand. As she'd done earlier in the evening, not so much as an eyelid flickered.

Faucon shifted to hold her palm to the light. The dark stain of dried blood marked out the lines and creases of her palm. There could be no question from whence it had come, when Waddard hired his brother to do his slaughtering so he and his wife could continue their work. So too, was the sleeve of her pale blue gown marked, the darker tint of blood hiding among the blotches left by the reddish clay she and Waddard shaped into vessels.

With all doubt destroyed, he returned to where he sat, yet staring through the door at the bit of the world he could see beyond it. He wondered if Juliana would have any recollection of what she'd done even when confronted with the truth. She'd removed Raymond's cloak but not his hood. Was that because she'd come upon the sack in which Dickie carried his clothing, garments she might have known even in her sleep? Or had she recognized his shoes and, thinking in her dreams that Raymond

186

had stolen them, reclaimed them for her son?

Outside the church, Etta appeared in the track. The old woman trotted swiftly toward Waddard's home. The speed at which she moved said she hadn't noticed her daughter leaving her last night. What she'd missed last night, she'd also missed the previous night.

Brother Edmund coughed himself awake. The monk rose and threw back his hood, then shifted swiftly toward Dickie's corpse. Edmund blinked in surprise as he saw the dressed corpse. He blinked again as he noticed Juliana curled next to her son.

Rubbing the sleep from his eyes, the monk came to stand next to his employer. "I thought you said you took his mother away from the church. When did she return to dress the body?"

"Juliana came in the dark of night, bringing with her Dickie's clothing," he said tiredly, looking up at his clerk.

"What?! She walked here alone in the dark just to bring clothing for her son? No woman does that," the monk retorted in disbelief.

"This one did. More than that, she walked alone in the dark with the boy's clothing while still asleep," Faucon told him.

Edmund looked askance at him. "That's not possible."

"It's possible for Juliana," Faucon countered. "Father Berold told me last night that she once worked for hours at the potter's wheel, asleep all the while. He said not even prayers or holy water were enough to wake her." Faucon sighed. "She murdered Raymond while trapped in her dreams."

Confusion flashed across his clerk's face. "But you said that the boy was pretending to be—" Edmund caught a sharp breath. His eyes widened. "Can this be true? His own mother?"

"Tell me, Brother. What does the law say about one who does murder without any knowledge that she's doing murder?" Faucon wanted to know.

Edmund's brows rose as he thought, then he shook his head. "Your question is akin to asking if she can be considered as deodand, at fault for the death, even though there is no possibility of the intent of causing death."

Here, the monk paused. His brows lowered. "But that's not what you're really asking me, is it? Sir, it matters not what the law says or doesn't say, not to you. You are only responsible for presenting the name to the jury for their confirmation and assessing the estate of the wrongdoer. This woman will have the same opportunity as any other accused of murder. She can bring her witnesses to testify to her character and circumstances when she's called to face our king's justice. Her guilt or innocence is theirs to decide, not yours."

"But I think when she learns what she's unwittingly done, she'll not survive," Faucon argued. "And if she dies before she can offer her tale, will I then bear the stain of her death on my soul?"

His clerk watched him for a moment, then tucked his hands into his sleeves. "You seek to carry more than is rightly yours. If hers is the name you must speak, it is because our Lord has so ordained it. If you doubt that, well then, that's a matter to set before your confessor. For the now, you must play the role the Lord God has given you."

Just then, the church door swung wide. Etta entered first, yet wearing her green gown. Her headcloth was tied haphazardly over her head. Her narrow face was pinched in worry.

"Thank the Lord! There she is," the old woman cried in relief as she saw her daughter sleeping at the back wall.

Jilly followed her grandmother into the church. The girl's fair hair went in all directions, yet tangled with sleep. Her blue gown hung slightly askew, as if pulled on in haste.

Her presence had Faucon on his feet in an instant. He met the girl at the center of the nave. "Come with me," he said to her, catching her by the shoulder, drawing her back to the doorway where they could be private.

As they stopped Jilly looked up at him, her face pale and her eyes wide. "Grandmama came crying that Mama walked away from her while yet sleeping," she said to him, her tone anxious and confused. "But how could Mama have done that?

She was here and you vowed to watch her. She is still here."

Faucon nodded. "I did as I vowed, and watched over your mother until she ran from the church. When I caught her, I saw that she was yet sleeping. Because your home was dark and your grandmother had met me in the track, I took your mother to your grandmother's house."

"Truly? She ran in her sleep? How is that possible?" the girl protested, not being old enough to have witnessed what her mother had done long ago.

"Jilly, your mother did more than just walk in her sleep," Faucon told her, then took her hand in his. "When the men of the jury arrive, I will have to tell them that Juliana of Mancetter killed her only son," he said gently. "I will also say that she did it while asleep with no knowledge of what she was doing. I cannot say what they will do after I say this to them. But if they do not refute me, they must confirm her name as Dickie's murderer. What concerns me is how your mother will react when I make my charge," he told her.

Jilly's chin began to quiver. The fear that filled her face said she had more than an inkling of what might happen when her mother was confronted with the truth. "What should I do?" she begged of her Crowner.

"Would that I knew," Faucon replied, speaking the truth that had gnawed at him since Juliana's return to the church. "But here is what I do know. You are stronger than you believe. Each day will bring its troubles, but there's one thing of which I'm certain. Nothing will ever break you, Jilly."

These words were all he had to give her. There were the ones he'd needed to hear but hadn't, when he found himself at a similar crossroad.

She stared up at him for a moment, then drew a steadying breath. When she left him, Faucon stayed in the doorway, watching her cross the nave then kneel beside her waking mother. He prayed he might have made her path a little easier.

Dies Mala

"Sister Cellaress, the sun sets. Why are we continuing on? We must turn back," Lady Marianne tells me, her tone concerned.

The girl sits atop the little donkey I brought to carry our baskets. I both asked for the beast and put the child atop it to please my heart. Our holy Mother also rode such a beast and the little lady is the image of our Virgin.

The child believes she rides to guard the baskets and the precious wax we purchased but an hour ago. In all truth, short of the animal falling, there's little chance of spillage, not when we travel the Street. The ancient roadway is raised, smooth and straight as an arrow.

"There's no need to be anxious, Lady Marianne," I say to her, seeking to assure. "We are always safe in our Lord's hands. Our destination is only a little farther."

I smile as I say this, while deep within me concern stirs. This was not the day I'd promised Him for my final sacrifice. Today is Dies Mala, an Egyptian day, one that showers misfortune upon the unwary. I remind myself that I am neither unwary nor did I have a choice. My holy task has already waited too long.

The day Lady Marianne and I made our brief visit to the village baker, who had no wax after all, I fell in the uneven roadway, reopening some of my wounds. When Mother saw the blood that stained my habit upon our return, she confined me to the infirmary. There I remained, trapped and anxious until midday today, a full five days later, and three days past my promised arrival at His gates. Although I prayed, so He might know I had not forsaken Him nor the task He entrusted to me, I've felt His presence waning with each passing hour.

Then I remind myself that no matter what I sense, it was

clearly His hand that arranged for our presence on the road right now. Not only did Mother agree to me leaving the abbey with the child when half the day was already gone, but she allowed me to go without Simon. But then, the hamlet I named sits less than a mile from our walls.

"Please, Sister Cellaress, let us turn back," the little lady almost pleads this time.

"Have faith, my child," I tell her. "Sing with me. Let us sing praises to our Lord as we travel."

Although concern continues to mar the perfection of her face, I lift my voice into the glorious words of *Veni Creator Spiritus*. She joins me after a moment.

The sun hung low in the western sky as Merevale's priest intoned the last blessing and made the final sign of the cross over Dickie's body. Standing with Faucon across the open grave from him, Brother Edmund nodded his approval. "That was perfectly done, Father."

"We could not have done it without your assistance, Brother," Abbot Henry replied for the priest. When he'd heard the true tale of Raymond's visitations, and that Mancetter now lacked a competent priest, he'd insisted on bringing his convent's priest to officiate at Dickie's burial. "Your suggestions for prayers were a Godsend. I'm certain we've warded off all the evil that might have sought out the dead boy. More than that, I believe the boy will rest easily, without suffering any of the anger or confusion that could cause him to stir the way his father once did."

Here, the Cistercian abbot offered a grateful nod to his Benedictine cousin. "How fortunate we are to have one who understands the walking dead well enough to advise us."

"Boys," Aldo said at the same time.

The lads who'd joined Dickie in his mummery stepped forward, shovels in hand. Although burying their dead friend had been included in their penances, it was also a labor of love.

All of them were red-eyed as they worked. They, along with Aldo, and Jilly and her sisters, were the only folk from Mancetter to attend Dickie's interment.

Two days had passed since the men of Helmingford Hundred gathered to confirm Juliana's name as murderess, four days since Juliana had learned what she'd done in her sleep. Since that moment she'd not spoken or moved voluntarily, and Etta refused to leave her daughter's side.

As for Waddard, he'd closed himself into his workshop, where he sought to do the work of two despite his hip. Faucon's appraisal of their assets had shown the family could ill afford the royal fine, should Juliana be adjudged guilty by the justiciars. The potter took consolation in the fact that there was little chance of the Eyre arriving in Warwickshire this year, or even the next. All that had left Jilly as the sole parent to her siblings.

Faucon watched as the girl herded her sisters out of the churchyard. They passed Alf and Will who stood with their horses and Edmund's donkey. Like Faucon, Will was also fully armed.

As Brother Edmund turned to make his way to the track, Abbot Henry hurried to catch Faucon. The Churchman rested his hand on his shoulder. "You are questioning yourself again," he said quietly. "I can see it in your face, my son."

"Why would I not?" Faucon replied, his voice equally as low. "The truth I found offered no one justice. But have no fear." He did his best to smile at the abbot. "I've taken your words to heart. I am certain that all is exactly as our Lord wishes it to be. Now, will you allow us to escort you and your priest back to Merevale?" he added.

The Churchman shook his head. "Father Guillame and I feel we must stay the night here with Father Berold. We hope he'll accept our offer to come to Merevale as a pensioner. I and my brothers are better suited to care for him, while his removal from Mancetter will free the Norman brothers to offer his benefice to another."

The abbot paused to shake his head. "Given what's

happened here, and the departure of Father Godin, these folk need a competent priest more than ever." To Abbot Henry's credit, he hadn't pressed Faucon for Godin's story when told of the Northerner's unexpected departure.

"You and yours must now be on your way," the Cistercian continued, casting his gaze heavenward. "By the sun, I think there's just enough left of this day for you to reach Nuneaton before full dark, if you ride swiftly."

As the abbot said this, Aldo left the lads to their labors to join Faucon and the Churchman. "Many thanks, my lord abbot. Your intentions for Father Berold are a great kindness, both for him and for us."

The reeve offered the Churchman a humble nod, then also bent his neck to Faucon. When he again met his Crowner's eye, he offered Faucon a small smile.

"Sir, I pray I need never again call for you to come to us. That said, all of Mancetter is fortunate that you were at the abbey when our need arose. Because of you, we are at last free of Raymond. Regardless of what it cost us all, that's a blessing beyond any value."

Faucon struggled for something to say but found nothing. He settled for a nod and a smile, then followed Edmund to the track. Within moments, the four of them had ridden beyond Mancetter's southern bound, splashed through the River Anker, and found Watling Street.

Heyward had said the Street would be hard to miss. The old man was right. Raised more than a foot above the ground, the grassy surface was unbelievably even, without holes or obvious ruts. Wider than two wagons abreast, it cut across the landscape without the slightest curve for as far as he could see. Taking advantage of the width, Will and Edmund brought their mounts alongside Faucon. In deference to his betters, Alf continued to ride just behind them.

"So this is where Harlequin's army rides," Will said, looking about him as if he expected to see the army of the dead appear at any moment. For once there was no snide edge to his tone. But then Will had spent the last four days tending to Father

Berold's needs, doing so by his own choice. This was so unlike the man his brother had become that Faucon worried at first. However, as each day passed Will seemed calmer, more settled in himself.

"Walter Map is clear, Sir William," Brother Edmund said, speaking across his employer to Faucon's brother. "It's Herla who rides here, not Harlequin. While their tales are similar, they are not the same man. Harlequin and his army collect those among the newly-dead who have blackened their souls during life. These corpses are made to suffer terrible and diverse torments for the whole while they walk with his army. However, once they've paid for their wrongs, they win their freedom. It seems no one is immune to Harlequin's call. Those who have witnessed his army say they see not only lewd women and common thieves among his horde, but also knights, lords, priests, and even bishops!

"That is not so with Herla," the monk continued. "He was once an ancient king in our land, a Briton. It's said this king was traveling toward his home when at a crossroads he met a faun, a Pan—"

"A little man, but still a king in his own right, although his realm was underground," Alf corrected from behind them.

Edmund ignored the commoner "The faun approached Herla, who stopped to speak to the strange creature. This Pan knew who the king was. He predicted that Herla would soon wed with the daughter of a king. Then he told the great warrior that when the wedding took place, he would attend the celebration.

"And so it came to pass, and Herla won the hand of a king's daughter. On the day of his wedding the Pan appeared with a great retinue. So many were there that Herla feared he'd fail in his duty as a good host. But the Pan had brought his own foodstuffs, and even his own service, and enough servants that Herla's own folk had naught to do.

"At the end of the celebrations, the Pan tells Herla that he himself will be wed in a year's time, and that Herla should attend. Herla is to come to the crossroads where they first met, and the Pan will guide his party into his realm.

"And so it comes to pass. The Pan leads Herla and his men into his realm. There they say for three days, enjoying the wedding celebrations. When Herla's party prepares to depart, the Pan gives Herla a dog to be carried on horseback out of his realm. He warns that no man should return to earth before the dog dismounts.

"When they are once again under the sun, and within the boundaries of Herla's holdings, riding upon this very road," Brother Edmund pointed to the Street, "they meet a man walking toward them. Although the man is strangely dressed, Herla asks him for news of his queen."

Here, Edmund paused to look from Faucon to Will and back again. "This man was like Father Godin, speaking a tongue that Herla can barely comprehend. That is because the man is a Saxon, not a Briton," he explained, then continued with his story.

"With much effort Herla understands this rustic is telling him that Herla is now a king of ancient legend. Herla, the man himself is told, disappeared with all his retainers and left his new bride to rule his realm.

"This so astonishes the great king that he almost dismounts. He remembers the Pan's warning just in time. The dog yet sits unmoving in front of him in the saddle. But another of his men is not so fortunate. He dismounts. The instant his feet touch the earth he dissolves into dust.

"So you see," Edmund finished, "Herla must ride for all time, or for as long as he wishes to retain his life, doing so because he sinned against our Lord when he dared to have dealings with pagan things. Harlequin, however, marches with his army to deliver rightful punishment to the wicked dead, no doubt to right his own stained record with our Lord."

"That's not the story I've been told," Alf again dared to correct. "Our tale says the little king from beneath the earth arrives at Herla's wedding bearing a great number of gifts, even though he's warned Herla he'll stay for but one night and leave before the sunrise. But when Herla comes to celebrate the little king's wedding, he comes almost empty-handed. This insults his host, who is a magical being. The little king curses Herla with eternal life for as long as he rides. And, at least according to my mother, Herla, like Harlequin, does gather the newly-dead to him. Those who have witnessed the Herlething's mad ride—"

It was Will's turn to interrupt. He looked over his shoulder at Alf. "Herlething?"

"It's the English word for Herla and his retainers as one," the commoner offered, then continued. "Those who have witnessed the Herlething ride often recognize their own recently-deceased kin among the horsemen."

Brother Edmund made an impatient noise. He also shifted to look behind him at Alf, although his gaze never actually fell upon the man. "And you've seen the ancient king as he rides?" he asked, his tone haughty.

"I have not," Alf admitted.

The monk sniffed, sitting straighter atop his little mount. "Then perhaps we should leave the details to those who know better."

Despite himself, the corners of Faucon's mouth twitched. Such was his life at the moment, filled with both Brother Edmund's snobbishness and his unwitting kindnesses, with Alf's grounded good sense, and with Will's unpredictable rages.

The sun had reached the horizon behind them, for their shadows now stretched far ahead of them on the Street. This when he gauged that at their slow pace, they weren't quite halfway to Nuneaton. It would be full dark before they reached the convent.

"Sir, did you hear that?" Alf asked sharply, pulling his piebald mount to a sudden stop.

As Will and Brother Edmund rode on, Faucon reined Legate to a halt. Frowning in concentration, he listened. Faint but clear, he caught a child's panicked cry.

"Huh, there must be some settlement nearby," Brother Edmund called back, yet allowing his little mount to proceed.

Faucon hesitated. Most likely the monk was correct, and

this was nothing. But when he tried to urge Legate forward the sadness in his soul— and a selfish need to make something in his world right— wouldn't allow it.

He scanned the landscape in the direction from which the call had come. For a furlong or so the earth was flat and grassy, then rose slowly for another furlong into a slight hill. Trees and thick brush cluttered the hilltop. There was no sign of habitation, no fields, no smoke curling into the sky.

"Wait here," he told the others as he kicked his courser into motion.

An instant later, Will brought Legate's brother alongside Faucon's mount. Again, the child freed a wordless cry. This time there was no doubting that the cry had come from the hilltop. Together, Faucon and Will shifted their horses to follow the sound.

"I will not remove my gown! You'll take me back this very moment!" shouted the yet-distant girl. She spoke in perfect French, her words filled with all the command given to one who might one day direct her own servants.

That had Faucon glancing at Will. But his brother had already put his heels to his horse, urging him to greater speed. Above them, the sky was now the deep blue given to ebbing twilight, shadows closing slowly around them as their horses huffed in exertion.

They were close enough now that Faucon caught the voice of the one to whom the girl spoke. Husky, seeming too deep to be that of a woman while not deep enough to be male. Although he made out none of the words, the tone made it clear this one sought to cajole.

"I don't believe you," the girl retorted loudly, her commanding tone tinged with fear.

"But you must believe," her captor replied, if this was a captor. "Our Lord has spoken to me. He has showed me that you are to come serve Him in His holy house. You'll not go alone. I'll also make this journey—"

The speaker broke off as their horses crashed into the thick brush at the top of the hill. "Where are you?" Faucon called.

"Here, here!" the girl shouted in return, then gave another panicked cry that ended in a gasp.

He and Will rode into a glade ringed by trees, among them several aged oaks. Branches loomed over them, whether trapping or protecting Faucon wasn't certain. Tied to a bush was a donkey laden with baskets. It sidled and huffed as they entered.

At the center of the glade stood a nun. She was tall, taller than Faucon, and broad-shouldered enough that she seemed manly. The nun had a simple white shift over one thick arm, while the other trapped the girl close to her. Despite that, her captive scratched and kicked.

It was this bold persistence Faucon recognized when he hadn't remembered her voice. "Lady Marianne?" he called in astonishment.

Then his gaze returned to the white shift over the Church-woman's arm. His eyes narrowed as long-stored pieces suddenly shifted and fell into horrifying place. "What is this?" he growled, dismounting. "You'll release the Lady Marianne immediately, Sister."

This cannot be! Never have I been interrupted during a sacrifice. I choose my sites with care to prevent just that. Then disbelief dies into something more horrifying. For these knights to not only find us, but to also know the little lady can only mean one thing. Our Lord has refused my last sacrifice.

Frozen in despair, I watch the knight come to earth. He wears his helmet over his chain mail coif. I can see naught of his face save the shadowed hollows of his eyes, the rise of his cheekbones, and his bearded jaw.

"Sir Faucon," the child cries as she writhes against me, seeking to break my hold. But I cannot let her go. To do so is to acknowledge that my heavenly Father has damned me for all eternity. Is this the price to be paid for my failure? But I have not yet failed Him! All I need do is complete the ritual.

The knight stops just beyond my reach and draws his sword. His stance promising death. I know better. To kill one avowed to God is the worst of all sins, and his life will be forfeit.

"You," he says to me, "you are the one who stayed in the church at Haselor. You took that child. You are also the one who left that murdered lass to the ravens outside of Prior Holston, as well as those I'm told came before her, before my arrival here."

Across the glade, the second knight's horse frets and turns. The rider's gaze never moves from me. The child in my embrace squeals. She thrashes and kicks. I bear her assault without flinching, yet swimming in a sea of disbelief.

How can this man know what I've done? For the first time today I consider that I have been careless, and also unwary, having committed those errors long before I knew to be cautious. Such is the action of Dies Mala.

"Our Lord accepted those girls as His. I but do His bidding," I tell the warriors with little hope they can ever understand. Such men are murderous brutes with little in the way of education, especially in religious matters.

"You will give her to me," the knight in front of me commands.

"She is no longer mine to give," I tell him. "I have promised her to Our Lord and He has accepted her."

"You'll release her now," he again commands, taking a threatening step toward me.

"Kneel with me, child," I tell the little lady, forcing her down in front of me. I settle on the grass behind her and bow my head. "We must pray for our heavenly Father to clear the way for our journey."

Pain explodes on the side of my face. My nose spurts blood. Gasping, I topple backward, taking the child with me as I fall. Then the knight is beside me. He grabs the arm I hold around the little lady, then bends my fingers in the wrong direction. I cry out in pain. Against my will, my arm weakens. I cry out again as the child is ripped from my hold.

The knight backs slowly away from me, his sword lowered. He cradles Lady Marianne on his left side. She sobs into his mail-clad shoulder, her arms and legs wrapped around him.

I free a heartbroken cry at the sight. His touch has already extinguished the light that revealed her as the image of our Holy Mother. Now all I see is her degraded future, her ruin and her ultimate damnation.

"You have no right to take her from our Lord. He has chosen her for something much greater," I plead with the armed man, wiping the blood from my mouth and nose as I struggle to sit up. "She is the embodiment of holy purity. Your touch befouls her."

"Will," the knight says to the second knight, "bring Brother Edmund here to me and swiftly so."

In an instant, the mounted man is gone, crashing back through the brush. Now there is only one! Desperation has me shoving myself to my feet. I am taller than he, and surely stronger. I am stronger than many men.

I throw myself at him, reaching for what is rightfully mine. His shoulder slams into my midsection, driving all the air from my lungs. My feet leave the earth. I fly back and fall to earth with such force that inner darkness threatens to consume me.

Gasping and gagging, I struggle to hold onto consciousness. But across the glade the knight has moved to his horse. I watch helplessly as he sheaths his sword, still holding the little lady. Prying free of her hold, despite her fearful whine, he sets my precious sacrifice into his saddle.

I lift myself on quivering arms. My stomach seeks to empty. "Stop," I gasp out.

"I'll be back for you," the knight warns me, mounting behind the child, rearranging her until she sits crossway in his lap.

Does he think I will stay when he takes what now belongs to our Lord, something that I need more than life itself? Driving myself to my feet, I stumble weakly after him. A gust of cold air sweeps past me. It's strong enough to rattle branches and send a shower of dry, dead leaves down upon me.

The little beast of burden that carried the precious lady tosses his head and stamps his feet. He turns and turns again, yanking at his knotted reins. I push past him and into the brush. I cannot fail. I must have my sacrifice.

"Who is she?" Faucon asked, even though he already knew that answer. If she'd done what he believed, she was a murderess many times over, one who deserved to die, but wouldn't. Her life belonged to the Church and the Church would jealously guard her life. If this was the sort of justice their Lord required, He was no sort of God at all.

"Sister Cellaress from the convent," came Marianne's broken response. She yet clung close to him, her arms wrapped tightly around his waist despite his mail tunic. "I thought she was my friend. But she isn't. She told me that I must die to please our Lord. I didn't want to die," the little lady sniveled.

Faucon closed his eyes with her words. His remembered image of the child with the slit throat on that grassy hillside shifted until it was this child he saw in the other's place. Just then, a blast of frigid air battered at him. He hunched his shoulders against it, allowing his cloak to fall forward and shield the child in his lap.

Letting Legate find his own way through the brush, he kept his arm tight around Lady Miriam's daughter. All thought of waiting in the glade with the nun until Edmund arrived ended when the big woman raced at him. It wasn't possible to protect the child while fending off a murdering nun. It wouldn't matter to the Church what the sister had done, only that he'd killed a Churchwoman.

"Pery!" Will shouted.

Faucon frowned when he found his brother. Rather than racing to fetch Brother Edmund, Will had stopped at the base of this hill, at the edge of the grassy sweep of land between the hill and the Street. With the moon long since risen and now more than half full, his brother's mail gleamed in the darkness. Nuncio's white hide was almost as bright.

Wondering why Will had stopped, Faucon looked toward the Street, only to have his gaze catch on two shadowy riders making their way toward Will. Alf and Brother Edmund, riding at a pace the monk's little mount rarely achieved.

Behind him, brush crashed. Twigs snapped. He looked over his shoulder expecting the nun, but it was the donkey. It exploded out of the foliage, raced past Legate, then turned in the direction of Nuneaton, no doubt to find its own way home.

The nun followed more slowly, limping. Her arm was clutched to her midsection. In the moonlight, the blood from his blow looked black where it stained her face and white wimple.

"You must give her to me," the nun pleaded. Now thick with tears, her husky voice sounded even more masculine. "I can save her soul. She's yet pure. Let me send her to our Lord while she remains untouched. I promise she'll stand with the angels as is her right."

"I don't want to stand with the angels. I want Maman," Lady Marianne whimpered and pressed her head more closely to his chest.

"Pery!" Will shouted again, his tone urgent.

Faucon kicked Legate into a walk, aiming his mount toward Will. He didn't bother looking to see if the nun was yet behind him. She would follow. He had what she wanted.

Dried grasses rustled. Then she was beside him, her hand on his foot in the stirrup. Faucon gave Legate the signal. Just as he'd been taught, the courser turned and came at the woman in threat. Although no destrier, he could kill with the right blow. She gave a startled cry and released Faucon's foot.

Then Legate stopped on his own. His head lifted, his attention shifting into the distance beyond the nun. His ears pricked. When he snorted, the sound was filled with question. His hide quivered, then he began to snort and sidle, trying to turn to the south as if he intended to follow the escaping donkey. Frowning in surprise, Faucon calmed his courser.

A piercing series of whistles shattered the still air. It was Will, giving their signal for imminent danger. Startled, Faucon looked toward where Will had been, but his brother, Alf, and Edmund were riding up the hill at all speed.

Wondering what drove them, Faucon looked back toward

the Street. "Holy Mother of God," he breathed.

As sheer as a rich woman's wimple, ghostly riders began to appear out of nothingness, their mounts stepping onto the Street, walking out onto that raised path as if their hooves were substance rather than shadow. He watched, incapable of moving, beyond thinking.

The riders— some bare-chested, others seeming fully clothed— sat astride. Their saddles lacked stirrups and the feet of the mounted men dangled below the bellies of their mounts. Every man carried an oval shield only slightly smaller than Faucon's own kite-shaped one. For weapons he saw spears and short swords belted to every side. Some had bows slung across their shoulders. Although a few wore metal helmets most did not. Those who didn't had hair so long that most wore it tied back the way a woman might.

Despite their uncanny transparency, he made out features on some of their faces. A chill raced up his spine. Although the army moved in an eerie and complete silence, individual riders shifted and turned, clearly speaking to one another. One man's mouth opened wide as he laughed soundlessly.

"Why is it so quiet?" Lady Marianne asked in a bare whisper. Rising out of her crouch against him, she craned her neck. But Faucon's cloak blocked her view of the Street.

Legate snorted, then shifted and kicked. There was the unmistakable crack of breaking bone. The nun screamed, the sound echoing in the silence. She fell to the ground, thrashing in agony.

In the road, the revenant army froze instantly. They didn't pause the way a living army halted, horses bunching and shifting as each man found his mount a comfortable place to stand. Every horse simply stopped moving, mid-stride, every man in whatever position he was in with that breath.

Once again, a frigid stream of air flowed over Faucon. This was no natural gust, nor was it winter's chill he felt in its touch. This was like the breath of some ancient god, one as cold and eternal as the grave.

The icy air curled around him, twisting and writhing. He

gagged as it seemed to reach into his chest. Lady Marianne gasped at the same instant. Behind him, the nun's cries abruptly ceased.

Faucon tried to shift in his saddle to see what she might now intend. Instead, like the army, he was locked in position, incapable of movement.

Behind him, brush rustled and shifted. Unbelievably, the woman was rising. Even more impossibly, he listened to the regular rhythm of her footsteps through tall grass as she made her way down the hill.

Frozen as he was, he couldn't see her until she was almost at the Street. Another chill worked its way down his spine. Although he'd heard her bone break, she walked in an easy stride.

Without hesitation, she stepped up onto the roadway and into the ranks of the frozen men. The instant her back foot left the earth, the army burst into frantic motion. Horses galloped, men raised their shields. They shook their spears as they threw back their heads and howled their soundless battle cries. Those at the forefront disappeared a short way down the Street while yet more ghostly soldiers streamed out of the nothingness to make the same short race.

And then they were gone. Faucon sucked in a deep breath, feeling as if he'd not filled his lungs throughout the whole experience. Lady Marianne tentatively stirred against him.

"I couldn't move," she sighed, sagging in relief.

"Ha!" Brother Edmund shouted, his mount shifting beneath him in surprise.

Again, the monk shouted, "Ha!"

Then Faucon's well-educated clerk stretched out his arms, threw back his head and offered a laugh that sounded like the cackle of a triumphant chicken. This from the man who thought he might have to kneel before a walking corpse and pray for heavenly intervention.

caught red-handed

Once again, Faucon sat in the chamber set aside for Nuneaton's male visitors, with its richly-curtained bed and strangely-constructed hearth. As he had the first time he'd visited here, he'd brought his stool close to the forefront of that strange hearth. This time, he hadn't needed an abbey maid to tell him to open the shutters on the narrow windows across the chamber so smoke would exit up the brick channel above the fire.

Will sat to his right on the second stool. Alf was at Faucon's left, seated on the edge of the straw-stuffed pallet he'd use as a bed tonight. The long-legged Englishman had cocked a knee and braced his arm upon it as he stared into the flames. The chamber was warm enough that all three had stripped to their braies. Since then, none of them had said a word.

As for Brother Edmund, the abbess had offered him the use of her private office as a bedchamber. He'd accepted eagerly, wanting both a prie-dieu and isolation from the women of the house. It also gave him the privacy to indulge himself in his overwhelming exhilaration over their experience, as expressed in uncontrolled outbursts of that cackling laughter that had marked their journey to Nuneaton. Faucon wondered if their Lord was being subjected to yet more of those outbursts.

Beside him, Will drew a deep breath as if rising out of sleep. He shook himself, signaling that he would be the one to break their silence. He looked at Faucon. "Do you believe what the abbess told you? Can such an abhorrent creature exist?"

Sudden and wicked amusement exploded in Faucon as the question brought by the entirety of what had just happened to them. Something that was as much a cough as a laugh escaped past his lips.

Only Faucon had been allowed beyond this chamber and into the abbey, and then only because Marianne refused to release him at the gate. He had taken her to the abbess, who had pulled her free. At that point, the child became frantic, unable to calm until Faucon promised to ride directly to Blacklea and return with her lady mother on the morrow.

Once the child had calmed, the abbess demanded an explanation. He hadn't given her the truth, not yet being comfortable with it in himself. Instead, he'd said only that the depraved nun had fled into the night and disappeared. That was when the abbess shared the true nature of the strange nun, doing so in the anger and frustration of being forced by her bishop to take such a creature into her house.

"Will," he said to his brother, "how can you even ask that question after what we've just seen?" Another amused cough escaped him. Fearing he would soon begin to cackle like Edmund, he pressed on.

"If we've seen Herla's army in their Wild Hunt, why can there not be a creature that is both male and female in one instant?" As he said that, Faucon's world once more came together, all the broken pieces Juliana's unwitting murder had created now finding their rightful place.

He drew a steadying breath, and saw what had been hidden from him and was now revealed. His Lord had seen to it that Abbot Henry's summons had drawn him to where he'd been most needed, not by Mancetter, but by the Lady Marianne. And Faucon had recognized their Lord's hand, guiding the murdering nun into that ghostly army for her rightful punishment.

It was a message, a sign, that he might not always see the scales balance, but balance they would. That was enough. Wicked amusement again bubbled up in him. He didn't try to swallow it this time. Instead, he threw back his head and let it free.

a noce from denise

I hope you've enjoyed my Medieval zombie story. Let me say that this story took me by surprise. While I knew that the Medievals believed that the dead walked, it was just something I knew. No story spark arose until I ran into a fascinating book: Afterlives by Nancy Mandeville Caciola. I started reading and, as has happened so often when I'm indulging in study, the characters and tale stepped out, fully formed. Of course, immediately after that I ran into an archeologist's report on bodies that showed evidence of having been exhumed and dismembered to prevent further walking on their part.

Also, for the record, I know little to nothing about the Wild Hunt and Herla's army. I gave myself permission to extrapolate because, hey, ultimately I am a fiction writer. I know how to make stuff up even if I don't do it very often.

Complaints, questions, praise? Please feel free to contact me at denise@denisedomning.com or visit my website at denisedomning.com (but be prepared to be confronted by a farmer's life.)

glossary

This book includes of number of Medieval terms. I've defined the ones I think might be unfamiliar to you. If you find others you would like defined, let me know by email at denise@denisedoming.com, and I'll add them to the list.

Braies:
: A man's undergarment. Made from a single piece of linen that is tied around the waist with a cord. Worn more or less like a loin cloth but more voluminous so the garment can be arranged to cover the hips and thighs.

Chausses:
: Stockings made of cloth (not knitted). Each leg ties onto the waist cord of the braies.

Crowner:
: From the Latin Coronarius, meaning Servant of the Crown. The word eventually evolves into 'Coroner'

Deodand:
: Derived from the deo dandum, meaning "to be given to God." An object is declared deodand if it is used to kill someone. The inquest jury is responsible for appraising the object's value and the owner is expected to pay a fine equal to that value. If the owner cannot pay, the hundred or village must pay in their stead. Theoretically, once the crown has taken possession of a deodand, it must sell it then use the profit for a religious or pious purpose.

cauᵹhᴛ ʀᴇð–hanðᴇð

The Eyre: The justices in Eyre. The noblemen and Churchmen who serve the king as judges. These men travel from county to county, hearing the pleas of the Crown. Years can pass between appearances of the Eyre.

Gambeson: A heavy padded, long-sleeved tunic usually hip length worn beneath a chain mail tunic

Hemp: A soft, strong fiber plant with edible seeds. Hemp can be twisted into rope or woven for use in making everything from storage bags to mattress covers.

Hundred: A geographic division of a county or shire. It likely once referred to an area capable of providing a hundred men at arms, or containing a hundred homes.

The Marches: Generally, the border between England and Wales. It is heavily fortified and heavily contested in the 12th Century. The Norman barons who rule the Marches are often referred to as Marcher lords.

Perry: Cider made with pears instead of apples.

Pleas of the Crown:

     To plead for justice from the royal court, or representative of the court. Like going to your local police station and filing a complaint.

Toft and Croft:

     The area of land on which a peasant's house sits. The croft, generally measuring seven hundred feet in length and forty in width. It was in the croft that a serf would grow their personal food staples, such as onions, garlic, turnips and other root crops, legumes and some grains.

Withe: A thin, supple willow (but also hazel or ash) branch

Printed in Great Britain
by Amazon